GENTLE TORMENT

Johanna Phillips

G.K. Hall & Co.
Thorndike, Maine

Published in 1996 by arrangement with Maxwell Lillienstein.

G.K. Hall Large Print Paperback Collection.

The text of this Large Print edition is unabridged.
Other aspects of the book may vary from the original edition.

Set in 16 pt. Century Schoolbook by Minnie B. Raven.

Printed in the United States on permanent paper.

Library of Congress Catalog Card Number 96-94382
ISBN: 0-7838-1859-9 (lg. print : sc)

GENTLE TORMENT

Chapter One

Lindy closed the door behind her and hurried down the hall, her footsteps echoed by the music and laughter from the party going on inside. She let herself out into the welcome silence of the long corridor that led to the office section of the camp. One of several in northern Alaska, the camp was built to accommodate the nearly one thousand workers who had come north to work for the oil companies and their suppliers.

A gas flare illuminated the area outside the ultramodern structure, and reflected in the small windows set along the corridor. The dim light outlined her gliding figure, slender, with short straight hair, almond-shaped eyes and delicate black brows.

When Lindy had first arrived, awed by the look of lunar landscape in the stark sophistication of the camp, she felt as if she was entering a space station of the future. Oblivious to her surroundings now, she unlocked the door and let herself into the office. The temperature outside was in the fifty-below range. The frigid wind swept the snow over the bleak landscape, but the office was warm and quiet.

Lindy was relieved to be away from the rooms she shared with three other girls, anticipating three or four hours of blessed quiet to work on her canvases.

When she first came north it had seemed an ideal situation to share the two bedrooms and sitting room. It was cheaper than a private room and, after all, she was here to make and save as much money as she could in the shortest possible time. The arrangement had been a learning experience for her and, although she was usually able to adjust to most situations, she couldn't get used to the new morality the girls seemed to take for granted. The party tonight was almost the last straw. The last thing she wanted to do was spend her evening sitting in the darkened sitting room fending off the advances of the sex-starved steelworker Peggy's friend had brought along for her. He tried to pull her down on his lap as she passed and grinned cheekily when she jerked away from him.

"What's wrong with you?" he asked curiously. "Why do you think I'm here? To look, but not touch?"

"You're not here by my invitation."

He tilted his head to one side, his long hair almost reaching his shoulder, and a smile of cynical amusement came over his rather good-looking face. Confidently unabashed, he lowered one eyelid in what he intended to be a flirtatious wink.

"Okay by me, doll. If you don't want to play there's plenty that do."

"Then I suggest you find them," she snapped.

He was undaunted. "You know, you're something else!" He stood up and tried to grasp her wrist.

"You're right. I am something else." She evaded him easily.

"If you're worried about the little woman, doll . . . don't. She's happy with the big check she gets every month." He grinned cockily.

"You're contemptible." All the scorn she felt for him and his kind was reflected in her voice.

"Yeah?" The smile said he was proud of it. "Maybe I am, but I'm not a frigid iceberg like you."

"It may surprise you to know that I'm not interested in what you are."

In the bedroom she packed her painting supplies in a tote bag and allowed herself one brief thought of Jake. How lucky she was that she discovered his true character before she was tied down with children like the wife of the conceited ass in the other room. Yet . . . at times her heart ached almost unbearably and she wished with all her heart that things could have been different for her and Jake.

Laying out paints, sketches and brushes in the office, she adjusted the light and was soon absorbed in her work. This canvas would be added to the growing inventory she was accumulating for the opening of her needlework shop when she saved enough money to go back home to Houston. Some evenings she painted in the small bedroom she shared with Peggy, but tonight she had received a broad hint the room would be occupied.

Time went so fast when she was doing the thing she loved most that it seemed she had been working only minutes when she heard the click of the doorknob. It would be Amos, her boss. When he guessed she would be here in the evenings he would come to work quietly at his desk, to be near her, to walk her back to her room later. Quiet, reserved and patient — also unmarried — he would be the ideal man for her . . . if she wanted a man. She shouldn't have let him start making love to her. He had kissed her — and it hadn't ended the way he'd so fervently desired! She was slightly ashamed, afterward, that she hadn't halted his ardent attempts sooner. She liked him, but that was all. He was good, sweet and kind to her, and she didn't want to hurt him. It was a problem she didn't exactly know how to handle.

Lindy wanted no attachments. She had had enough of philandering men to last two lifetimes: a father who made her mother's life miserable and a husband who broke her heart with his infidelities just months after the wedding. It had been like the end of the world for her, as if she had walked off a cliff, or been hit by a tornado. She had wanted to scream and tear her hair, but she had done neither of those things. She did the only thing possible for her to do. She left him.

"Hello, Amos." She wished he hadn't come. She wished she didn't know how he felt about her. Life could be so damned complicated at times.

There was no answer. No sound at all. The silence became obvious. Reluctantly she turned, ready to give him a tender smile to mask her feelings. Her gaze clashed head-on with the man standing there. She blinked. Oh, my God! Had she lost her mind? She took a deep breath and held it for an eternity while she stared.

"Disappointed?" The voice! It caused her spine to sag. She hadn't heard it for two years. She sat there stupidly, her emotions like a crazy seesaw, struggling for words.

"Jake?" she choked. He stood there looking at her. Why didn't he say something? "Jake! What are you doing here?"

"Why shouldn't I be?" As if that was sufficient explanation, he moved toward her, glancing around the room. Then he stood still again and stared at her.

She moved uncomfortably and her pulse raced under the intense scrutiny. He must be as shocked to see her as she was to see him. On the other hand he didn't appear to be shocked at all. Two years was a long time and a lot had happened to both of them. But . . .

oh, her eyes seemed glued to his face.

"This is a surprise." Her throat was tight and she just barely managed the words. Surprise wasn't the right word, it sounded so trite, but she had to say something.

"Is it?" Mocking words that dripped with sarcasm.

"You haven't changed!" she flared, finding release in anger. "Still as arrogant and impossible as ever." It had been a long struggle to erase his image from her subconscious. Night after night she had dreamed of him, despising herself for her inability to control her mind. Lately she had begun to believe she had escaped him, would never see him again. And now this . . .

"Leave it," he said coolly. "You've made your opinion of me clear. I didn't come here to start the war all over again."

He turned to remove his coat and hung it on the rack beside the door. He was a tall man; leaner and more muscular than in the old days. The mustache gave him a mature, worldly look, also missing in the old days. His light-brown curly hair was sun-streaked and his skin brown from a tropical sun. He was the only man she had ever known with hair like that and with ice-blue eyes that turned green when emotionally aroused. Although her love for him died when she discovered his betrayal, he still remained the most fascinating man she had ever known. She had been twenty-two and helpless with adoration. Now she was twenty-five and far more capable of assessing a man.

"How are you?"

"Fine." She didn't look at him. What the hell did he care? He hadn't been in touch with her in two years.

His eyes assessed her critically, moving over the short, shiny brown hair that fit her head like a cap to the widely spaced blue eyes with their dark fringe of lashes. His eyes narrowed as he gazed at her mouth and her lips trembled at the image that came swiftly to mind: Jake probing hungrily, Jake taking possession of her mouth. Letting his gaze travel to the firm breast rounding out the sweater she wore, he smiled a secret smile and she burned with resentment. Slowly, coolly he let his eyes roam over her from the narrow waist on down over slim hips and long legs to the tips of her boots and back to her eyes now sparkling with indignation.

"You're thinner."

She did her best to return his gaze coolly. What she really wanted was to tell him to get out and not come back. She felt tears close to the surface now. How long could she hold them back? Instead, she repeated flatly, "I asked what you were doing here, Jake."

"To see you. What else?"

"You needn't have come to ask for your freedom. I offered you that when you made it plain you needed more than one woman. Papers are waiting with your attorney. All you have to do is sign them and the proceedings will be started."

"Is that why you think I'm here? You're as far off the track as you ever were."

"You came all this way to tell me that?" Her bitter gaze locked with his while her mouth tightened with anger. "Well, you've said it. Satisfied?"

Jake raised dark eyebrows. "What are you doing in the office at this time of night?"

"It's none of your damned business." Defiance blazed in her eyes. "But if you must know, I'm here because it's quiet and I can work on my paintings."

"What paintings?"

"Needlepoint canvases. I plan to open a shop when I go back to Houston . . . if I go back to Houston."

His brows came together in a frown she recognized as one of displeasure and a little pleased flutter punctuated her already rapid heartbeat.

"I'm sorry about your mother." She didn't look at him. She knew he meant what he said. He had been wonderful to her mother. She would always owe him for that.

"Do you have a man in your life?" Jake could never be accused of being tactful if there was something he wanted to know.

"After my father? After you?" She looked at

him as if he had lost his mind. Her face was tight with emotion and her blue eyes, though slightly misty, looked defiantly into his.

"Bull!" He muttered the word, but she heard it. Almost casually he walked over to where her paintings lay on the desk. "Very good." He picked up a canvas and held it at arm's length. "A whooping crane?"

"Yes. I'm doing a series of birds." Her voice was strained.

"Have you turned frigid, Lindy?"

Her back stiffened with surprise and her head came up. Her voice, when it came, quivered with anger.

"What do you mean by that?"

"The party in your room. Why aren't you there?"

He heard her catch her breath and turned to see the color rising up her neck to cover her face.

"I'm still the prudish spoilsport I was, Jake Williamson! I still have a few old-fashioned principles. I don't smoke pot and I don't sleep around!" Her voice was shrill and didn't sound like her own.

"Regular saint, aren't you?" He made it sound as if it was something disgusting. "You've got some pretty tarnished friends, saint."

"They're not my friends. I was assigned to the rooms when I came here to work. They just happened to be here at the same time I am." Damn him . . . she didn't have to defend herself to him.

"Why did you come up here? You had a good job in Houston and the allowance I paid into your account was substantial." He picked up the stack of designs and looked at each one carefully.

"I took my personal account to another bank. The money you paid into the joint account is there waiting for you. I don't want it. I came here to make the big money, the same reason everyone comes here. In a few months I'll have enough to open my shop and I'll go home."

"The main reason you came here was to get away from your father so you wouldn't have to see him and his new wife." He said this casually while still looking at her designs.

She didn't answer and he turned to look at her stricken face. Her eyes were bright with tears. Push . . . push . . . push! Wasn't he going to leave her anything?

"I thought so. You see I know you very well, Mrs. Williamson."

She wanted to snatch her designs out of his hand and run out of this place. But the party wouldn't be over for several hours yet. And . . . how did he know about the party? Damn, damn him! He'd always been able to figure out everything about her; how to touch on just the right nerve to stir her up to say things better left unsaid. In the three short months before they were married and during the six

16

months they lived together they had shared every thought. With him she had reached her greatest happiness and her greatest despair. After two years she had adjusted to life without him and here he was again, in living color, and with no effort at all, he was stirring up emotions she had long thought dead.

"Don't you have a girl waiting for you, Jake? Waiting in some dingy little apartment?" She wanted to pierce his calm shell.

"Is that what you thought of ours, Lindy? A dingy little apartment?" She ignored him and was shocked at the bitterness in his voice when he added, "Why do you ask? You didn't want me."

"I never ran with the pack, Jake."

"Don't rake over old coals." He was upset now. Had she finally gotten to him? "And to satisfy your curiosity, I've got women stashed all over. I'm a regular Bluebeard! I take four to six women to bed every day and a dozen virgins on Sunday!"

She sucked in her breath and bent her head as if concentrating on her work, but was intensely aware of him moving about the office.

"Tell me about this company."

"Amos Linstrom is the manager. I'm sure he can explain the company better than I."

"I doubt that. What's your job?"

"Same work I've always done — bookkeeping, payroll, tax, log sheets and anything else that needs to be done."

"What's in the thermos?" His way of changing the subject was so familiar she didn't even stop to think about it.

"Hot cocoa, but I only have one cup." She shook the bottle. The action was unnecessary. The bottle was almost full.

He grinned. "I don't mind."

She poured the steaming liquid, but made no move to hand it to him. He picked up the cup and turned it to the spot where a faint trace of lipstick was visible. Looking directly into her eyes he ran the tip of his tongue lightly over the rim of the cup before he drank. His eyes sparkled at her, his lips twitched in an effort not to laugh. He was flirting with her, but it wasn't going to work! Lindy felt a small impulse to smile indulgently at his efforts.

"You still haven't said what you're doing up here." She tried to make her voice sound casual, uncaring.

He ignored the question and asked one of his own. "Is there anyplace open where a man can get a meal?"

"The bar and restaurant never close."

"How about coming with me?"

"No."

"Afraid to come?" he taunted.

"Why should I be afraid?" She deliberately chose to misunderstand his meaning. "You may want to cut my throat, but you won't."

"You know what I mean. Are you afraid you

may have some feeling for me after all this time?" His tone was teasing.

"You flatter yourself."

"You may as well come along. It's too early to go back to your room." He was laughing at her now and not even trying to hide it.

"No." Picking up her pencil she bent over the sketch, but her hand was too rigid to move.

"Suit yourself." His eyes raked her then rested on her trembling lips. After a full thirty seconds to take in the sight of her he turned and shrugged into his coat and she had to suffer another going over by those piercing blue eyes. Then he was saying in a demanding, grating voice, "Stay here until I get back."

A burst of almost hysterical laughter rose in her throat. It was unbelievable, but there he stood . . . commanding her! She glared at him defiantly. Her feeble attempt to defy him was short-lived. His eyes narrowed and his mouth compressed into a grim line.

"Well?" he demanded through clamped teeth.

She swallowed and nodded her head and hated herself for doing it. He opened the door and went out.

That one grated word almost shattered her control. Tears stung her eyes, but she dashed them away impatiently. She had done enough weeping over Jake Williamson: she wasn't going to let the tears start again, no matter what happened. Although he hadn't said so there was only one reason why he could be here — he had met someone else and was ready for the divorce. Two years was a long time for a man like Jake. Time for him to meet dozens of women. Then the thought crossed her mind that he wouldn't have come all this way if it was just a divorce he wanted.

The shock was evaporating now, but deep tremors of unease still chased through her body as she was forced to relive those days of agony, when each day seemed to stretch like an eternity.

The only child of an unhappy, mismatched couple, Lindy had known from an early age her parents had problems. She had watched her mother become sullen and withdrawn as the years went by. She didn't remember ever spending a weekend, during her childhood, with both her parents. In later years her mother lived in a small world of her own, a fantasy world where she was happy and content.

Hers had been a story-book romance. Jake owned a small transport company and they met when he came to the office where she was employed by a friend of his. "Lindy and Jake," he had said. "I like the sound of it. We go together." They had been drawn to each other as steel to a magnet and married a few months later. He was everything to her. Jake was Jake. He was kinder, smarter, sexier, more

20

loving and understanding than she had imagined a man could be. She firmly believed he would never hurt her, be unfaithful, disappoint her. Lindy understood things like unfaithfulness and disappointment after watching her father flaunt his "flings," grinding them into her mother's heart until he broke it. They had a private language, she and Jake. They laughed at each other's bad jokes, remembered things that mattered and were inclined to accept each other as they were. He was hers. Her husband, lover, best friend.

There had been nothing unusual about the beginning of that day, nothing to warn Lindy that a change was about to twist her life. In the months to come she would clearly remember everything that happened, every little minor detail, and relive them over and over again.

She sat in the living room long after the girl had left. She was waiting for something. Something that would make things right again. This couldn't be happening. Not really. Jake would come home and it would be as it was yesterday, last week, last month. He knew how she felt about being faithful. The girl claimed he had stayed with her each week when he went through Orange, had done so for months, had made her pregnant. She was in love with him, had gone off the pill deliberately so she would get pregnant, sure he would marry her. Jake! Oh, God, no! He had broken his promise! He had come home to her after sleeping with another woman. He had pretended love for her. Oh, God, she had to find out for sure. But who would tell her? Liz? Liz had worked for Jake for several years. Lindy didn't really like Liz. There wasn't anything she could put her finger on. Liz seemed to be too possessive with Jake, but she was an ambitious woman and that could account for it.

She drove to the office, her desperation making her reckless and oblivious to the horns that blared their irritation as the small Pinto sped through the streets. She ran up the steps of the loading dock, burst into the office and confronted the cool, smiling, attractive blond whom Jake had dubbed his "right arm." When she left a half hour later, her body weary, her mind tortured, Liz's words were ringing in her ears.

"I'm sorry you had to find out this way, Lindy. All the fellows know . . . just go out and ask any of them. They'll tell you it's true because they do the same. It's the nature of the men on the road. Don't take it so hard, honey. You'll get used to it. No one woman is ever going to satisfy Jake. That's why I didn't encourage a permanent relationship with him. Go on back home and make a good dinner. You'll have him most of the time."

A wave of sickness rose in Lindy. Liz didn't care at all that her world had crumbled. Was she imagining that Liz looked pleased? Liz and Jake? No! Jealousy was causing her to lose her mind.

"Most of the time . . . most of the time." All the while she was throwing her things in a case the words went through her mind. Tears almost blinded her as she wrote about the girl from Orange who was having his baby. On her way out of the apartment she dropped the note on the kitchen table.

She had gone to Debra, her friend of many years, the only person in the world she could turn to. Debra had urged her to see Jake, to confront him with his betrayal, but she had refused and locked herself in a room while he banged on the door with his fist. She lay on the bed, rigid, her fist pressed against her mouth.

The doorknob went sailing across the room an instant before the door flew open. Jake set the large sledgehammer beside the door and came toward her. There was nothing warm or soft about the expression on his face. He stared at her for a moment without speaking. The savage flame in his eyes spoke for him.

"You would take the word of some cheap floozie over mine?"

"Do you deny you've slept with her?"

"No," he said heavily. "I can't deny that."

The admission felt like a dagger plunging into her heart. She looked at him with quivering torment, hatred in her eyes.

"You could go to . . . her after me?" Anger dried her tears. "Do you expect me to ignore what you've done? I'll hate you till the day I die for doing this to me." She was shaking uncontrollably with the desire to hit him.

"I was with her one time. Before I met you." His eyes were sharp and narrow, searching her face. He had made a flat statement. She could either believe him or not.

"You forget I've seen her, talked to her. I've . . ." She broke off there. A tiny ray of hope had begun to burn in her heart. His words were so simple, so sincere. He hadn't played on her love for him, or made elaborate denial.

"Do you believe me, Lindy?" She saw the tremor pass over his face. His eyes fastened onto her eyes. "Lindy?" He sounded ill, but he couldn't be. She was the one dying inside.

Her throat hurt. She swallowed. "I want to believe you." There was shock and pain in her eyes.

"Darling," he whispered and sat down on the bed. "Darling," he said again as she abandoned her pride and went into his arms. Her eyes were damp, but no more than his. This was the Jake she loved. He felt so good, smelled so good. He felt and smelled like Jake. She was home. They kissed again and again with a hunger that made them shake.

"I was scared, babe. I was so damned scared I'd lost you." He rocked her gently in his arms. "Life would be damned lousy without you." He took a deep breath and held her tightly to him as he slowly stroked her hair.

"I love you." There were tears in her eyes and in his.

"I know, and I love you." He looked down at her, smiled tiredly and whispered. "Let's get out of here and go home."

Jake opened the door to their apartment, clasped her hand and led her through the darkened rooms to their bedroom. Once inside, they reached blindly for each other, each wanting to love and be loved, possess and be possessed. Wherever he touched her, Lindy felt sweet waves of desire, at first gentle, then growing in urgency as they tasted and savored each other. Finally, with his arms holding her firmly, insistently, against him, together they felt the world fall away as they reached that ultimate moment of ecstasy. Afterward, her face buried in the curve of his shoulder and neck, inhaling the familiar smell of him, they lay side by side, touching, kissing, murmuring to each other.

After a time Jake said gently, "You've got to know, honey, that girl couldn't possibly be carrying my child." Lindy wanted to believe him. She had to believe him or lose her mind. "She was in the office today when I got back from Dallas. I recognized her, but didn't know the mischief she'd been up to. She's just a girl, sweetheart, who travels the highways in a motor home with a citizens'-band radio. One night, in a rest area, she crawled into the cab with me and, feeling in the mood, I took what she offered. When I realized how young she was I gave her some money and a stern lecture on the dangers of highway soliciting. It was before I met you, honey. Long before I met you. I don't know how she found me, but I don't owe her a thing. Not a damn thing!"

Lindy tried to banish the incident from her mind, but the oneness they had shared before was missing. Jake was attentive and his whole attitude indicated that he felt the misunderstanding was behind them. Lindy, on the other hand, had a deep-seated ache in the center of her body, a jealous ache she recognized with reluctant dismay. She wanted to be immune to it, but every glance, every softly spoken word that passed between Jake and an attractive woman brought it all back.

The days of wine and roses were over. The heady bliss of life with Jake was being destroyed bit by bit. Lindy, tormented by jealousy, realized that Jake had no idea what his flirtatious ways were doing to her. Still, she could not help what she felt. She was hungry for possession of every little corner of her husband's heart and resentful of any other demands on him.

It all came to an abrupt ending on the night the company held a welcoming-back party for one of the drivers who had been injured and spent several months in the hospital. It was

Liz's party from beginning to end. She reserved a small darkened room at the Holiday Inn, ordered the food, the drinks, and arranged for dance music. She shone, glittered in a skin-tight evening pants suit. She played the hostess, seeing to everyone's comfort, especially Jake's. Liz, all smiles and fluttering lashes was treated by Jake with a teasing indulgence that pricked at Lindy's heart. The men teased, fondled and danced with her while Lindy and the other wives sat quietly by and danced only when their husbands asked them. By one o'clock Lindy wanted to go home. Jake wanted to stay. He and Liz had been giving their version of dances from the thirties and forties. It was evident they had danced together quite a lot.

"Don't be a party pooper, sweetheart." Jake stood swaying, one arm flung across Liz's shoulder. "I can't leave yet." He had drunk far too much. Lindy had never seen him this drunk before.

At two o'clock she left alone. She went to bed tense, filled with anger and jealousy, but sleep overtook her anyway. When she awoke it was five o'clock and she was still alone. Slipping out of bed she went down the hall to the living room and the image of what she found there haunted her day and night for months; Jake, his face flushed in sleep, his hair tousled, lay entwined with Liz on the couch. His head was pillowed on her bare breast. The girl smiled triumphantly as she looked across the room at Lindy.

Lindy gave a choked gasp of pain as if a knife had been plunged into her stomach. She knew, of course, it was the end. Jake had sworn fidelity and she had tried to believe him. Her own blindness now infuriated her.

When she came out of her bedroom carrying a suitcase Liz was dressed and sitting in a chair beside the couch.

"Bye," she said softly.

Lindy checked into a small hotel, wildly furious at being caught in the same trap as her mother. Jake relayed messages through Debra that she was childishly immature to kick up a fuss over one drunken spree, that she should have enough love for him to forgive and forget. Lindy lost all hope and filed for divorce, sending him word she never wanted to see him as long as she lived.

Shortly after that a card came in the mail. It was unsigned and simply read, "Never is a long, long time."

Jake left the country almost immediately. Her lawyer sent the necessary papers to his lawyer to be forwarded for his signature and each time she had inquired she received the same answer. He had not been able to locate Jake.

Fighting to regain her composure before Jake returned, Lindy dried her eyes and reapplied her makeup. Determined to stay aloof, she intentionally brought to mind the picture of the young girl standing nervously in the doorway of their apartment. The picture of Liz and Jake on the couch was too painful, too humiliating to remember.

She heard the door open and close, but didn't look up from her desk. Jake took off his coat and came to stand beside her. He set a brown sack on the sketch she was working on and she was forced to look up. He drew up a chair, sat down, and moved the sketch to a nearby table. Ripping the sack down the side, he laid out sandwiches and french-fried potatoes.

"I only have one cup," he said and uncapped a styrofoam cup of steaming coffee. "We can share it."

She tried not to look at him. He was deliberately antagonizing her.

"Eat," he commanded. "You're beautiful, but too skinny."

"You're taking a lot on yourself." She had had all his arrogance she could take. "A . . . mistake from my past trying to change my eating habits."

He was silent for so long that she looked up and surprised the shadow of pain in his gaze, then his eyes narrowed.

"You think that's what I am? A mistake?" She had touched a raw spot. Resentment burned in his eyes.

"What else would you be, Jake?" She enjoyed

seeing him on the hook for a change.

"Lover?" He was back in control.

"Certainly not!" Angrily she pushed the sandwich across the desk toward him.

He laughed aloud. "You've become bitchy, little pussycat. It doesn't suit that angel face." The sandwich was back in front of her. "Eat and stop hating me. I'm not your father."

"But very much like him!" Sparks of anger glittered in her eyes.

Jake expelled a heavy breath and reached out and grasped her wrist. "Don't ever say that to me again."

His sharp words whipped her like a lash, and tears sparkled on her long lashes. The blue circles from her previous weeping were already painted under her eyes. She shook her head and started to say something. Her mouth opened and she closed it again. She took a breath and braced her thin shoulders defensively.

"Regardless of what you think about me, never again tell me I'm like your father. I'm me, Jake Williamson, and nobody else."

She turned her face up to meet his accusing stare. She had regained a measure of control, and although her eyes were still swimming with tears, her mouth was taut and there was an air of unconscious dignity about her poised head.

"You're a ... bastard, Jake." The words came out quietly.

"Don't talk like that. The Lindy I knew would have never said that!" Now he was the one who was ill at ease.

"That Lindy is dead, Jake. You killed her. I'm no longer the stupid, trusting little soul you once knew."

His gaze flicked to the set, defiant face, then to the red marks his fingers had made on her arm.

"You're talking nonsense and you know it." Her slender fingers whitened as they gripped the cup she was holding. Her wide gaze traveled to his face. "Can't you accept my apology?"

She betrayed surprise at the question. "For what?"

"Not for what you're thinking," he said curtly. "I didn't mean to grasp your arm so tightly."

She stared steadily at some point beyond him as she said slowly, "It's all right. I don't break easily."

He rubbed his fingertips slowly back and forth across her arm. She wanted to jerk it away, but darned if she would let him think his touch bothered her. She forced herself to allow it to lie still. Keeping her eyes averted, she was aware of his close scrutiny. Her heart pounded like that of a scared rabbit and she was sure he could feel it beating through the fingertips on her arm.

She sensed, rather than heard, him sigh. He got to his feet.

31

"Party must be over by now. I'll walk you back to your room."

"That isn't necessary."

She rolled the remainder of the meal on the paper sack and placed it in the waste container and stuffed her art supplies in the tote bag.

Jake was waiting with her coat. She slipped her arms into the sleeves. With his hands on her shoulders he turned her around and deft fingers worked the buttons on her coat. She stood perfectly still. His movements seemed to be very slow and deliberate. Before she realized his intent or could prevent it he bent his head swiftly and kissed her gently on the lips.

This unexpected action took her by surprise and she jerked away from him and picked up her bag to cover her confusion.

"Don't . . . do that!"

"Okay." He was good-naturedly amused.

He turned out the light and hesitated just a moment before opening the door. That minute seemed an hour to Lindy, not knowing what he was going to do. Whatever it was, he changed his mind, and they went out into the cold corridor.

The rooms were quiet, the sitting room dimly lit, when they reached it.

"The party is over, or they've gone to bed." He would think of that, she thought dryly.

"Good night." It was dismissal.

He took the knob out of her hand and pushed the door open, following her into the room. It showed signs of the party. Glasses on every table, cigarette butts filled the ashtrays and bits and pieces of food on the table and floor. Lindy caught him eyeing an undergarment that had been tossed into a corner. She wanted to laugh. Jake had never been embarrassed in his life!

"Which room is yours?"

She indicated the room. He went to the door and flung it open.

"What the hell ya want, Yank?" a slurry Southern voice called.

Jake slammed the door. The thundercloud look on his face was laughable.

"Where will you sleep?"

"On the couch. I've done it before." Something in the amused tone of her voice made him frown even more. "You can get a room in the bachelor quarters."

"I'm no bachelor. Remember?" He was looking at the two sofas at the end of the room. "Got any extra blankets?"

She stood helplessly in the middle of the room, not knowing exactly what she was going to do.

"Did you reserve a room?" She wanted him out of here.

"Didn't need to. My wife has a room. I'm tired, Mrs. Williamson. Where's the john?"

While he was gone she made a feeble attempt to clean up some of the mess from the party, but realizing it would take hours she abandoned the job and spread the blankets on the sofas.

Jake came back into the room, sat down on one of the makeshift beds, removed his boots and stretched out.

"Just think, this morning I was in Houston. God, but I'm tired." He looked at Lindy and his lips twitched. "Here I am, spending the night with my beautiful wife and I'm too tired to make love to her." He laughed as she stalked to the bathroom.

Chapter Two

Lindy's head was pounding. She was unable to get her thoughts together, she was confused, tired, and wanted desperately to go off somewhere and cry. It was as if her heart had been pounded to a pulp and her mangled emotions heaped on top. She felt limp and drab as a pile of wet laundry. Her only escape was to force her numb mind to concentrate on her work. Even that was difficult. Betty, the junior clerk and the only other woman in the office, was a pert blond just out of business college. She had come north thinking there was a woman shortage, sure she would land a rich, handsome husband. She spent her evenings at the disco looking and her mornings telling Lindy what she had found. This morning was no exception. She had rattled on insistently.

Amos came in, grunted a greeting, and went into his private office. Lindy's brain was so full of turmoil it didn't occur to her to wonder why he didn't pause for his morning chat.

The door opened again and a rush of cool air from the corridor hit her back. She knew who it was for Betty perked up immediately.

"Hello." She was practically purring. "What

can I do for you?"

"It depends on what you have to offer." The familiar voice was mocking.

Betty laughed. "Would you like a dossier?"

"Complete with pictures?"

"Absolutely!"

Lindy refused to acknowledge him. Let him flirt with a featherbrain like Betty. It came as natural to him as breathing.

"Introduce me to your friend, Lindy."

"Jake Williamson meet Betty Haver."

"Williamson?" Betty exclaimed. "William-son? Same as yours, Lindy? Any relation? Long-lost cousin, maybe?"

Jake's eyes, sparkling with deviltry, went from Lindy to Betty's flushed, excited face.

"Do we have a family resemblance?"

"Hardly none at all." Betty was almost panting.

The heat of anger passed through Lindy. She knew, without looking up, that Jake was watching her reaction to his little flirtation. Her fingers moved swiftly over the calculator while she waited for him to drop the bomb that they were married. He knew what she expected him to do and chuckling at her discomfort he trailed his fingers across the nape of her neck as he passed on his way to Amos's office. "He's a dream, Lindy!" To a girl like Betty he would be.

"Yes, he is," Lindy murmured aloud and then to herself, "a nightmare."

"Tell me about him. Will he stay around for a while?" The petite blond rattled on, not waiting, or expecting an answer. It left Lindy free to settle into her work.

When Amos and Jake came out of the office she turned to the file and pretended to be selecting a folder.

"Lindy, Betty." Amos cleared his throat. "Mr. Williamson is the new owner of the company."

"How exciting!" This from Betty, of course.

"He plans to merge this company with two others he owns and that means there will be a lot of extra work. During the next few weeks we will be changing procedures. You will be paid double for all overtime."

Jake's eyes never left Lindy's face while Amos was talking. She was aware of this and proud she was able to keep from crying. It seemed her stay in the frozen north had come to an end. She would never work for Jake!

Amos stood silently after making his announcement. Betty let go a stream of gushing comments that made Jake laugh. Lindy bent her head over her work.

"I've got some things to do, Amos. I'll be back later and we can go over a few things. Okay?"

"Sure, Mr. Williamson. I'll be here."

"Jake. Call me Jake. No one calls me Mr. Williamson except my wife when she's mad at me."

Amos went into his office and Jake went out. Lindy could see him jogging down the corridor as her desk was in line with the door. He hasn't changed, she thought. Hasn't changed one little bit. Still flirts, still jogs, still has an eye for business.

"You didn't tell me he was married," Betty wailed. "Oh, for goodness sakes! Maybe he's separated or divorced. I hope so!"

"May I see you for a moment, Lindy?" Amos stood in the doorway.

Lindy followed him into his office, glad to get away from Betty, but one look at his glum face told her he was anything but happy. He waved her to a chair then seated himself behind his desk and fumbled with the papers stacked neatly in front of him.

"Wasn't really a surprise. I knew the company was being sold, but didn't expect the new owner to show up so soon. Seems to be a right kind of guy. Knows what he wants and insists on getting it. I've heard about him. They say he can truck anything, anytime, anywhere, and after meeting him, I believe it. What I can't understand is why you didn't tell me you were married." He looked at her now. His face was tight, almost as if he faced an enemy. Christ! She hadn't thought about Amos.

"Amos, I . . . I didn't think it was important. We're getting a divorce." She hated having to explain even to Amos who had been kindness itself. A resentment welled up inside of her. She had made it plain to him from the start that she was not interested in a personal relationship and if he had hoped for more she was sorry, but it wasn't her fault.

"Not according to him you're not." His voice now held resentment.

"We're not what?"

"Getting divorced. He said you were working out your problems and he . . . warned me off." Amos's face reddened. "He said if I had any notion of having an affair with you to forget it."

"He said that?" Lindy was trembling with anger. "Damn him! What I do is none of his business and we are getting a divorce!"

Amos stood up. "I'm only telling you what he said, Lindy. I'm sorry you didn't tell me yourself. I have become . . . fond of you. You're the only woman I've met since my wife died that . . . that I've wanted to be with. I'm disappointed." His brown eyes seemed to plead with her, expected her to say . . . what? He ran his hand over his perspiring forehead and thinning hair. When she didn't speak he said with resignation, "If and when you decide what you want and if I fit into your plans you can let me know."

"Amos . . ." She went to stand beside him. "I'm sorry if . . . well, if you're disappointed. I never wanted anything more than your friendship. Please believe that."

His face lost its stern lines and he smiled. "I know that, Lindy." He took her hand. "If you need a friend, I'm available."

"Thank you." Somehow her eyes were misty and she blinked rapidly. She took his hand in both of hers and squeezed it tightly.

The door opened and Jake stood there, his narrowed eyes going from one to the other and then down to their clasped hands.

"Anything pressing to be done this morning, Amos?" His voice was clipped, impersonal. "I'm taking my wife for a couple of hours."

"Nothing I can't handle. I'll send the payroll cards out, Lindy. The plane leaves," he consulted his watch, "in about half an hour. Go along, I can finish them in plenty of time." Amos released her hand, but not before he held it in both of his. The act was deliberate and Lindy secretly applauded his courage.

Betty sat with her elbows on her desk, a mutinous look on her face. She had heard Jake refer to Lindy as his wife and the high hopes she had nurtured for a new affair were dashed.

Lindy took her coat from the rack, grabbed up her purse and walked rapidly out the door ahead of Jake. When they were several yards down the corridor she turned on him.

"What the hell do you think you're doing coming up here and interfering in my life, telling Amos we're going to work out our problems?" Her chin was lifted and there was rebellion in every line of her body. "Do you really have the . . . gall to think you can come here and I'll drop all my plans and take up

40

with you again? If you think that, you're the most conceited wretch I've ever known."

For a long moment he stood there, his blue-green gaze locked with hers, while her voice lashed him with bitter, unguarded words.

"We are not getting a divorce."

Lindy closed her eyes. Had she really heard that appalling statement? The stark words hung on the cold air. Anguish worked in her face, threatening to break through her control.

"You won't have anything to say about it. After a certain length of time I won't need your signature." She trembled with the force of unspent emotion and backed away from the cold fury in his eyes.

"I'll fight you to the last ditch to keep our marriage intact." He stood on spread legs, his arms folded across his chest.

"Why?" she gasped. She was truly shocked.

He watched the emotions flick across her face. For a long moment he searched her anguished features, the mouth set so tight it was colorless, her eyes bright with anger and unshed tears.

"Because I choose to." The words had more meaning because they were softly spoken.

Her mouth twisted bitterly. "It's a pity you were not born a sultan. You would have been right at home with a harem."

He unfolded his arms and laughed. "You're being childish. I suppose you're still sulking over my . . . indiscretions."

"Don't tell me you're going to deny them?"

"I wouldn't attempt to do so."

"I'm past sulking, Jake. I'm tired of you hanging about my neck like an albatross. I want to be free to plan a future without you in it."

Cynicism curled his mouth. "I never thought you would still be so prudish, my sweet. Seems I got here just in time. Your . . . friend, Amos, almost dropped his jaw when I told him you were my wife. What's wrong for me is okay for you, eh?"

"You're impossible! Amos and I never . . ."

"Given time you would. For God's sake grow up!"

Lindy tried to control her shivering and failed. She stared at his dark, mocking visage. She took a deep breath.

"Why did you come here?" Suddenly Lindy's stomach lurched. She felt like throwing up.

His mood changed abruptly. "To see my wife. Husbands and wives should be together. I know that now. I made a mistake going away. You can bet I'll not make that mistake again. Remember it's Jake and Lindy. Lindy and Jake." He smiled down at her as if they had never exchanged a harsh word. "Come on." He took her arm. "Don't pout. We have work to do."

Lindy allowed him to propel her down the corridor. She was so wrung out from the emotional scene that she went through the line at the cafeteria in a daze. She followed Jake to a table by the double thickness of glass that made up the wall of the building. At one o'clock in the afternoon it was almost dark here at the top of the world. The gas flares which gave off an eerie light burned continually. The biting wind swept across the snow-packed surface with a boldness that would sweep your breath away if not for the protective shield of the heavy glass. A snowmobile roared past the window, the driver buffeted by the wind.

"It must be seventy below out there." Jake said.

Lindy glanced at him accusingly; she couldn't have possibly put all that food on her tray! He ignored her glance and went to get the thermo-pot of coffee from the service bar.

They ate in silence. The food rolled around and around in Lindy's mouth before it would go down. She avoided looking at him and focused her attention on the other diners. Amos and Betty came in and went down the line together, but sat at separate tables. Betty gave her a definite snub as she sailed past and for the first time all day Lindy wanted to smile.

Jake caught the slight lift to her lips and his eyes held hers in conspiratorial amusement. Her heart gave a sudden sickening leap. The ability to read each other's thoughts and to communicate without words was still there.

She looked down to hide the knowledge he was sure to read in her eyes. She understood the bond between them, just as she knew that the almost unbearable longing that swept her at times was more than a physical need. But none of it would make any difference to their relationship. It was better to remember her true motive for leaving him, to steel herself against the dangerous knowledge that his lips, his arms, his masculinity, the whole essence of him could make her long to surrender on any terms. Giving way to moments like this could only lead to more heartbreak. Jake would take all she had to give, and her own need, her own pride, would be swept away like so many grains of sand. A shudder ran through her limbs and with trembling hands she picked up her bag and got to her feet.

"Thank you for the lunch," she said as if thanking a business acquaintance. She forced a composure she was far from feeling. "I must get back to the office."

"Afraid the new boss will fire you?" His blue eyes were darkly amused.

"He won't have to. I'm giving notice." It was the only defense left to her now.

"Well, in that case . . ." He was cheerfully confident. "Come along. We got a chore to do."

With a firm hand beneath her elbow he ushered her out of the cafeteria and toward the living quarters. She clamped her lips tightly together. Not for anything would she ask him where they were going. They walked silently down the long darkened corridor, her legs working furiously to keep up with his long stride. They stopped at the door to her room and he held out his hand for the key.

"What are you trying to pull now, Jake?"

"I'm not going to rape you, if that's what you're thinking. Although I'm not so sure it would be rape." His words shattered her composure.

"Stop this, Jake!"

The amusement on his face infuriated her. Nothing made her so mad as to be laughed at and he knew that very well. She turned to go back down the corridor, but took only a few steps and he was in front of her. The smile gone from his face.

"I've arranged for you to have another room. A private room where you can paint to your heart's content."

"I can't afford a private room. And I'll be here only a few more weeks. Only until you can get a replacement."

He shrugged his shoulders. "Another girl is already packing to move into this room with the girls. So give me your key, we're wasting time."

Angrily she slapped the key into his hand.

He followed her into the bedroom and they both stared at the disorder. Clothes of every description were strewn around the room, the bed was unmade and wet towels lay on the carpet. Lindy went to the closet for her cases. Long arms from behind her reached over and lifted them from her hands and put them on the bed.

"Let me help so we can get out of this mess. We have two choices. We can make several trips carrying this stuff down what would amount to five city blocks of corridor, or we can load it on a snowmobile and cut across to the other wing in one trip. Which shall it be?"

"Whatever takes the shortest time."

"I thought you'd say that." He grinned. "I've a snowmobile waiting."

She gave him a disgusted look and then her eyes fell on the box in the corner.

"I can't let my tubes of paint freeze."

"Leave the paints to me." He picked up the box and began to wrap the tubes carefully in a suit of thermo underwear he picked up from the pile she dumped on the bed. "How will you take your finished pictures?"

"They will lie flat in the suitcase."

"Be sure and leave out enough warm clothes for the trip over."

They worked quickly and silently together. The first embarrassment of his handling of her intimate things passed and it was almost as if time had rolled back to the days of their love. He always knew what she was going to do before she did it. Their understanding of each other was uncanny . . . up to a point. She begrudgingly admitted it was good having someone to help her. She was tired of being a loner, but being married to a cheat was worse!

Jake looked like a man who had walked on the moon when he came in after loading the snowmobile. He raised the ski mask and grinned at her before adjusting the mask over her face and pulling the fur-lined hood up and over her head.

The wind was blowing so hard it would have been impossible for Lindy to stay on her feet if not for Jake's arm around her. The roar of the Arctic blast crowded out the sound of the snowmobile engine. He lifted her in and slid into the seat in front of her. Gratefully she leaned her face against the shelter of his broad back. It didn't take but a few minutes for them to reach the other wing of the giant building, but in the blowing gale it seemed much longer. He pulled the machine into the wind shelter beside the door and hurried her inside before plunging out again to bring in the cases.

The room was big and square. It was furnished more tastefully than the other one. There was thick pile carpet on the floor and colorful slip covers on the couch and chair. Jake proudly showed her around. He pointed out a small refrigerator and electric burner, microwave oven, hidden cupboard with dishes and utensils and a small stock of quick to prepare food. There was no doubt that they were in the executive section.

"Jake, I don't belong here."

"Whatever gave you that idea?" He opened a door to allow her to glance into another room. "Here's the bedroom." It was small but beautifully furnished. "Bathroom is over there." He was trying not to grin. "It only has a shower, but you prefer a shower."

Her face burned. Slowly things were becoming clear to her.

"And who is going to occupy the other room?" My God! Why wouldn't he leave her in peace? Her face had gone from red to white and he was startled at the expression of despair in her eyes.

"Your husband, that's who."

"No!" She was painfully aware that his flat statement was a summing up of his intentions in more ways than one. At least she had no illusions about that. She went quickly to the door. His whiplash voice kept her from opening it.

"For God's sake, quit being such a prude!" He advanced a couple of strides and caught her by the shoulders. "Don't tell me that you're so unsure of your feelings for me you can't stand to be near me for a couple of weeks. If that's the case, Lindy, it tells me quite a lot."

His grip slackened and she spun around dreading that he should see the betraying tears. With a quick movement of his hands he forestalled the move and seized her arms. For a long moment he searched her anguished face, then released her abruptly.

"Lindy . . . Lindy, you're still a worrywart."

He unzipped his snowmobile suit and stepped out of it. His sun-streaked hair was ruffled. It looked glossy and healthy and brushed the collar of the turtleneck sweater that matched the blue of his eyes. He was not the most handsome man she had ever seen, but he was definitely the most masculine; lean, but with a powerfully built body. His eyes had always disturbed her the most. Between the longest lashes she had ever seen on a man, they seemed to look into her and through her.

Realizing she had been staring, she turned away. It was at moments like this she could imagine nothing had changed, that love still lay unspoken and the words he said so easily were to be believed. He knew she had no choice when he engaged these rooms and had blatantly taken advantage of the fact. What was she to do now?

Gently Jake pushed her into a chair and tugged at her heavy boots. She was too worn out to resist. Kneeling there, he took her stockinged foot in both of his hands and squeezed it.

"Warm feet, cold heart!" He laughed, his lips spreading to show even white teeth. The small wrinkles at the corners of his eyes had not been there before and as she openly studied his face the thought came to her that he was older, not the man she had known before, but a man not to be trifled with. He was hard and experienced, and yet at times she had caught a tender look in his eyes. Jake had a sentimental streak, if but a small one, that surfaced frequently during the time they were together. Possibly it included her, for old time's sake, along with his sister and her two boys.

He was still kneeling there holding her foot. "You're trying to decide if I'm a hero for getting you out of that place or a villain that's dragged you into his den of iniquity."

She smiled rather tightly. "Not . . . exactly." Her eyes shifted to the hands holding her foot. They were lean and brown and beautifully shaped. Strong, responsible hands, ruthless hands. She couldn't allow herself to become intimidated. Hands like Jake's held on to what they wanted, they took, they bruised . . .

"I've got to be getting back. The mail will be in and I'll have a lot to do."

His brows raised. "How about unpacking?"

"I'll do it tonight."

"I had other plans for tonight." And noting the sudden flare of her nostrils he hurried on. "While I was in South America I dreamed about a pot of Texas chili and a pan of golden cornbread. How about cooking it for me if I can scare up the makings at the commissary?" His brows raised in question. "Besides I want to see how you fill each one of those little holes

50

with yarn to make a picture."

"I want you to know that I've forgotten nothing, Jake. Absolutely nothing. Your vanity needs to believe that I'll come back to you, but I won't."

He didn't speak, only looked at her, defying her in silence.

She gave a twisted little smile. "Nothing to say, Jake? That makes a change."

"I'll walk you back. There's a network of corridors in this place. You might get lost."

It was late in the afternoon when Amos came by her desk and asked if she was settled into her new quarters. She told him she was and he went out toward the coffee shop. Lindy waited for a remark from Betty. She wasn't disappointed.

"Why did you keep your marriage such a deep, dark secret? Have you been separated? The girls will get a charge out of our Little Miss Priss being married to that man. How come you never mentioned him?"

Lindy was suddenly ice and daggers. "My marriage is none of your business, dammit, and I don't want it mentioned again. Do you understand? Furthermore, don't ever refer to me by that ridiculous name again."

"You don't have to get so huffy. I tell you about my affairs."

"That's right. You tell me. I don't ask you."

"Hello, girls." Jake stood in the doorway, his eyes compelling her to look at him. He held

51

her eyes and she seemed powerless to look away and wondered for the hundredth time how she could be attracted to a man who took her faith, her heart, her body and her innocence and then threw them away.

"You've worked long enough, sweetheart." His eyes held a roguish twinkle. "Let's go. It's been a long time since we've been alone."

Lindy burned and wished desperately for a way to deflate him. She grabbed her coat and took off down the corridor, anger speeding her steps. She didn't want to feel anything toward him. He had come back into her life when she was feeling particularly lonely and that accounted for the flutter in her heart when she was near him and she angrily resented it.

He walked easily beside her. "I got all the fixin's for the chili." She said nothing and he took her arm and slowed her pace. "You keep that up and you'll be worn to a frazzle by the time we get there."

"We don't have an oven." She stiffened her facial muscles and gritted between her teeth.

"I know that. We can cook it in the microwave or on the grill like hotcakes. Remember when we went on a picnic to Galveston and . . ." She turned her head and looked at the wall. She didn't want to hear what she knew he was going to say. "And I asked you to marry me."

When they reached the apartment she went through the sitting room to her bedroom and closed the door. She looked around for her cases. The room was neat as a pin. She opened the closet doors. Her clothes were hanging in a neat row — coats, slacks, skirts, dresses. Her shoes and boots were on the floor beneath them, empty cases on the shelf above.

With tight lips she went to the bureau and opened the drawers. Her underthings were neatly arranged. A quick glance at the dressing table showed her that her cosmetics were there. Her anger flared, then exploded when she saw her one and only filmy nightgown lying on the end of the bed.

Fighting the feeling of being on a roller-coaster she flung open the door and confronted him.

"How dare you handle my things!" She clenched her hands together so they wouldn't fly out and hit him.

Jake looked up from the small work counter in the kitchen, genuine surprise on his face.

"Now what's bugging you?"

"You know perfectly well what's bugging me, Jake. You know every trick in the book, don't you? It isn't going to work! Whatever your motives you can be sure of one thing, Jake Williamson, and that is I'm not going to allow myself to be taken in again."

He gave a bewildered shake of his head. "You've got yourself in a stew because I unpacked for you. This is the twentieth century, for chrissake! We've lived together. I've seen plenty of panties and bras."

"Of course you have!" She was mad clean through. If only the darn pounding of her head would go away so she could think clearly. "I want a divorce, Jake."

His eyes were disturbingly intent. "Do you?"

"You know I do." She brushed a hand across her forehead. "Why, Jake? Why did you come here?"

"You're a smart girl. You figure it out."

Lindy felt sick and empty. She wasn't prepared for the agony of confronting him again, but she was compelled to ask, "Are you here to tell me again the girl lied when she said you had slept with her and that you did not have an affair with Liz?"

"No. I'm not saying she lied. What I am saying is that I never stopped in Orange, Lake Charles, Dallas or any other town to look up a woman after I met you. You won't let yourself believe that."

"No, I don't believe that. A whore wouldn't have come to Houston to look you up, Jake."

"Of course you don't believe it. You're so full of your own self-righteousness you only believe what you see. Did it never occur to you to trust your husband? I got drunk that night and you went off like a spoiled kid. Liz brought me home. You wouldn't even believe Liz when she said that was all there was to it. She begged you to stay and let me explain and you wouldn't even do that!" Shaking from head to foot, the vision of Liz cuddled in his arms on the couch flashed before her eyes.

"She said that?"

"And more, but we needn't go into that." He brought a brandy bottle from under the counter and poured himself a stiff drink. "I've known wives to trust their husbands when they were accused of heinous crimes and all the evidence pointed to the fact they were guilty."

"Isn't it ridiculous to be so blind that you can't see the truth?"

"Perhaps my example is extreme, but if you love someone you usually give them the benefit of the doubt. In our case there was not enough love and too much doubt."

Lindy had to defend herself. "There was no way I could doubt that poor girl. She was distraught, desperate."

"My God!" He slammed his glass down on the bar. "You couldn't doubt her, but you could doubt me and we had lived together for six months."

"Not all the time."

"I was away maybe one night a week. Do you think I was so starved for sex I couldn't do without it for one night? The subject is closed, Lindy. I didn't come up here to start an argument over something that happened two years ago. Go take off your coat and let's get on with more pleasant things. And try, for once, to see things through your own eyes and not through the eyes of your mother."

Lindy had to admit that the evening was enjoyable. They prepared the chili together. He told her about the famous paintings he had seen in museums around the world. He was a stimulating companion and his knowledge of paintings, although recently acquired, was extensive. Lindy listened with interest in spite of herself, hungry to hear about places she longed to visit. She told him how she got started painting for needlepoint. Painting first for herself then for Debra and her friends, and finally deciding to branch out commercially. There was a sense of unreality in having him here, sharing in the preparation of the meal, talking to him as if two days instead of two years had gone by.

They shared the clean-up and afterward sat on the couch. He insisted she show him "how she filled all those little holes to make a picture." He stretched his long legs out in front of him, his head resting on the back of the couch. His eyes watched the rhythmic movement of her hands as she stitched.

"I've missed this." He let out what was a half sigh, half yawn. "It's what I missed the most, I think. The peaceful quietness, the companionship, the . . . just being with you. This is the way it used to be."

She went pale. His blue eyes darkened when she glanced at him. He looked tired, she thought. The hard bones of his jaws were clinched, and there were shadows under his eyes like bruises. The lines on each side of his mouth were lines of fatigue. Her breath caught in the back of her throat, but when she spoke she chose her tone carefully.

"No. This isn't the way it used to be at all."

He surveyed her through half-closed lids. "Maybe not, but you're still as tranquil as a harbor in a storm. You'll have to admit it's been a nice evening."

He drew her hand from the needlework and down between them on the couch lacing his fingers with hers. She began to tremble, the easy companionship of the evening was gone and in its place an alarm was sounding that the situation could get out of hand. She tried to pull her hand away, but he tightened his grip.

"Were you still seeing Dick Kenfield when you left Houston?" The question was delivered suddenly.

"How did you know about that?" Her heart was beating heavily.

"Were you trying to hide the affair?"

"No, but . . ."

"He isn't your type."

She looked up with wide-eyed disbelief and her gaze focused on his face, her mouth set in a grim line.

"Dick is a nice person, a really nice person, and if I thought you had anything to do with his being transferred to Chicago, dammit, I'd

. . . I'd . . . You have absolutely no right to interfere in my life, Jake. You really are impossible. Do you know that?"

"Think about it. He wasn't your type."

Lindy stared at him, dumbfounded, and he stared back as if he was not seeing her at all, but something that suddenly made him go pale and haggard. He was shaking, as if with a chill, breathing roughly, as if he had just completed a long run. Was he ill? She jerked her hand free and got to her feet.

"Don't move!" The words were sharp as a pistol shot and frightened her into pausing. He was beside her in two steps and his hands closed around her upper arms. She winced at the tightness with which he held her.

"Are you never going to listen to me? There's a limit to how far you can push me, Lindy."

"There's a limit to how far you can push me! I won't take much more! You can't dictate what I do any longer."

His face turned a deep red as their eyes did battle. Dragging her against him he lowered his head and fastened his lips to hers, kissing her bitterly, cruelly, hard, unloving kisses that took her breath from her. She struggled without success and finally surrendered to his superior strength. At last he lifted his head. His arms held her so tightly she thought she would faint and her blood pounded in her temples like the beat of a tomtom. She turned her hot, aching mouth to his shoulder.

Anger at her helplessness caused her to raise her head. "Do you think I don't know why you want me?" she said accusingly, hatefully. "It was a blow to your ego having your wife walk out on you. You've come here to punish me, to make me pay and pay and pay. You hate me, don't you, Jake?"

"My God, but you are blind . . . and stupid! You're the only person in the world I've ever loved besides my sister and you know that isn't the same."

"No!" She tried to push herself away from him. "You only want to hurt me more."

"You're damn right I want to hurt you." He was shouting now. "I'm human. You hurt me almost more than I could stand when you walked out on me, when you took the word of some cheap tart over mine."

"That wasn't the only reason I left you. She wasn't your only affair."

The words tumbled from his mouth as though she hadn't spoke. "When I left for South America I hated you so much I was sick. You stuck a knife in my guts and twisted all the illusions out of me. I thought I had found perfection and discovered it was as phony as a three-dollar bill."

"How do you think I felt? Still feel?"

"Still feel?" He laughed without humor and pushed her from him. "Go to bed, Lindy. I won't ask you again to believe in me. You don't know what trust means."

She stood with head bowed. She felt sick and empty and her head was going around and around. She had known that sooner or later she and Jake would have a confrontation like this but she hadn't prepared herself for the agony she would feel.

"I did what I had to do. The sooner you accept that what we had is over, the better off we both will be."

"Yes." His lips twisted. "We will, won't we?"

She watched him until the door of his room closed behind him. Her head was throbbing and when she bent to pick up her needlework she was so dizzy she had to hold onto the couch until the room stopped spinning. She turned off the lamp and with leaden feet went to her room.

Chapter Three

It seemed to Lindy it had been years since she had been alone. It was pure heaven to strip off her clothes and get into the cotton pajamas without stepping over Peggy's discards. She put away her pants suit, then dug into her purse for her sleeping tablets.

Before opening the door to the bathroom she listened for sounds of occupancy, then went in and shot the bolt on the door going into the other bedroom. The click of the metal resounded in the small room. She gave herself a quick sponge bath and filled a glass with water to take back to her room.

The room was unusually warm, or else her distraught nerves made it seem that way. She lay down across the bed and after a few minutes shrugged out of her pajama top. The satin spread felt cool against her breast. She lay with her head hanging over the side of the mattress staring at the floor, wondering why the knowledge that Jake slept in the other room didn't fill her with alarm. For the first time since she packed her bags and left the apartment in the middle of the night she allowed a figment of doubt to enter her mind.

What if Jake had told the truth? What if Jake had been so drunk he didn't realize he slept with Liz on the couch? That was no excuse! Jake was attractive to women. And he liked them! So . . . Her brain was too tired and too confused to think about it. Thank God for the sleeping tablets. She'd take a couple and her mind would find rest.

Blindly she reached for the bottle and the glass of water went crashing to the floor. In her haste to grab for it the bottle of pills rolled off the table.

"Idiot . . ." she muttered in frustration and a mist of nervous tears came to her eyes. She was straining to reach the bottle and the blessed rest it contained when the door was flung open. Jake stood there.

"What happened?"

She barely looked at him, but she knew he was coming toward her, was standing beside the bed. "I knocked my water glass off the table. Is that such a crime? Now would you mind leaving me alone?"

He picked up the glass and reached under the table for the bottle of pills. "What's this?" He held up the bottle, then opened it and poured the small, white, lethal-looking tablets out into his hand. "What are you doing with these?" His harsh tone almost petrified her. When she didn't answer he demanded, "What are you taking?"

She tilted her head so she could see him

looming over her and reached out her hand. "Headache tablets. Just give them to me and go!"

"I'm not stupid, Lindy." He looked down at what lay in his palm. "They're narcotics. A measured dose of narcotics that some like to refer to as sedatives — sleeping tablets."

"And if they are, what business is it of yours?"

"Everything about you is my business, you little fool, and this especially! How long have you been taking this stuff?"

She buried her face in the bed. "Not long. Only when I have a headache." She heard him set the glass on the table and looked up hopefully. He stood looking down at her and, as she watched, put the bottle into his pocket. She sighed and turned her face away. She sensed rather than heard him move away from the bed, and when she didn't hear the door close, opened her eyes. He was standing at the bureau with her handbag in his hands.

Without stopping to consider her bare breast she sprang from the bed and tried to snatch the bag from him. He turned his back on her and extracted two more bottles of pills and slipped them into his pocket. She could have scratched his eyes out so frustrated did she feel.

"Don't take them all! Please, Jake, don't take them all!" Her plea was almost hysterical. She flung herself at him, flaying him with her fist.

"I hate you, Jake Williamson! I wish I had never set eyes on you!"

He grabbed her wrist and held her away from him. He stared at her disbelievingly, his brows drawn together and his eyes narrowed into a green glitter. They stood like that for a long moment; his attention riveted to her anguished face.

"What has happened to you, Lindy? My God, you know better than to get hooked on this stuff!"

With a gulping sob she tried to wrench herself away from him, but his hands pulled her closer until his arms enfolded her and he pressed her wet face into the curve of his neck. Her control snapped and she begged pitifully, "Please . . . oh, please don't take them all. You can't know what it's like. The night is so long, Jake. It's like forever. I can't endure it . . ."

The anger died out of him. "Lindy . . . sweetheart," he murmured hoarsely. His hand ran up and down her body, slowly touching her, stroking, caressing. "Darling, darling, sshhh . . ."

All of her resolve had crumbled. She abandoned thought of everything but the sensation of being close to him and of the flurry of excitement his hands were arousing in her. Aware now of her bare breast pressed against the silky texture of his shirt, the muscles of his chest hard beneath, surprisingly she didn't care much what he did to her as long as she could be close to him like this. She wound her arms around his neck, inviting possession.

"Jake . . ." she pleaded. "I . . . the night is so black . . . so lonely." With closed eyes she lifted her mouth and offered herself to his possessing lips.

"For chrissake, Lindy. I don't want to take you like this!"

She gave a high moan, reacting with panic. "Please . . . Jake!" she whispered feverishly. "Please give me the pills."

His mouth covered hers with a hunger that silenced her, forcing her lips to open beneath his own. One hand moved up to hold her neck in a viselike grip, tilting her head so she could not escape from his passionate kisses.

"Oh, my God!" he muttered. "Is this another dream?"

They strained together, hearts beating wildly, and kissed as lovers long separated. His hands roamed restlessly from shoulders to hips and up to the delicate white glimmer of her breasts. He began to shake and his kiss became deep, deeper, until they both were dazed and breathless. His mouth still kissing her hotly, he lifted her into his arms and carried her to the bed. She kept her eyes tightly closed not wanting to come out of the tranced state, reliving the dreams she had of their nights together. Only now she was wildly, burningly awake, and as Jake's hands moved freely over her she felt the tightness of her muscles relax and the strain of the long, lonely months fade into nothingness. Her fingers moved in his hair as his head moved down her body, feeling the familiar thick, warm hair as his cheek brushed one of her breasts. His mouth gently slid over the white skin until it touched her nipple. Repeating the caress, his mouth became more seductive. His hands moved down her body pushing the thin cloth down over her hips.

Abruptly his hands fell away. She opened her eyes to protest. He was leaning over her, his lips a breath away.

"There's no turning back now, Lindy." The words seemed to be wrenched from him. "Don't tell me tomorrow . . ."

She stopped his lips with hers. "Love me, Jake. Don't think about tomorrow."

He clicked off the light and seconds later stretched out beside her on the bed.

"Don't think, my darling . . . go with the tide," he whispered. Lindy allowed her fingers to roam over his taut cheekbones, remembering the chiseled contours, and her desire was sparked anew with each touch.

It was all so sweet, so much better than she remembered. He was an unhurried, gentle lover, the stroking of his hands on her skin sent waves of weakening pleasure up and down her spine. He was invading every inch of her body, making her give herself up to him. She remembered the first time he had entered her. She had been scared and shy. She welcomed him now. Nothing mattered except her own desperate need for love.

The need for him blazed crazily in her brain. It was dangerous to give herself as she was giving to him now . . . she was vulnerable, asking for rejection, humiliation . . . pain. But she wouldn't think of that now . . . not tonight.

Her arms clutched him frantically as his mouth came down to her pulsing throat, kissing the soft skin. She arched against him tugging at his powerful body as his hands slid under her and she opened her thighs to receive him. His breathing came fast and irregular and his heart thudded above her as his movements quickened and he whispered softly, words whose meanings were muffled as he kissed her soft lips and his tongue probed at the corner of her mouth. The driving force of her feeling was taking her beyond reason, beyond fear, beyond herself into a new dimension. Her hands moved to his throat, slid over his shoulders, and her fingers curled in explosive excitement into his thick hair.

He drew his lips away and buried his face in her throat, kissing it hotly. There was a frenzied singing in her blood and it grew with such rapidity that the words beat against her brain. "Let it last . . . let it last." She heard sounds of his smothered groans as if they came from a long way to reach her ears and then the pleasure rose to intolerable heights and she was conscious of nothing but her own sensations. She felt herself floating down weightlessly and she clung to Jake's shoulders, the only solid thing in the unbalanced world.

She fell into a warm, lazy, languid silence, which was like peace on a summer day at the beach. Jake's head dropped onto her shoulder, his breathing slower, his heart quieter. She lay passively, her arms twined around his neck, while his hands stroked her body gently. The feeling of panic and tension was gone. She had meant to give to him the fulfillment of his desires as well as to satisfy her own. And now she hadn't the necessary courage needed to move away from him. She fought to block out everything but this moment . . . this night. She snuggled against him, her arms locked about him, and sleep overtook her like the dark cloak of night.

Artificial sunshine, issuing from a sophisticated indirect lighting system, awakened Lindy in the morning. Her mind slowly became aware of the disturbing glare. It intruded, shining through her closed lids and penetrating into her brain. She stirred sleepily as a hand began to caress the small of her back.

She lay without moving, dazedly aware that this was an unusual awakening. Then she became alert, realizing she was pillowed on Jake's bare shoulder, lying naked next to his strong, warm body and inhaling the very presence of him. She lifted one hand and delicately touched the hair on his upper lip. Under her fingers the hair was soft and prickled pleasantly. The gold-tipped lashes parted and he looked down into her face.

Her body lay still against him while his hand continued to stroke her back. For a long moment they merely looked at each other.

"I'd forgotten how beautiful you are first thing in the morning." His hand moved to push the dark fringe of hair from her face.

A sigh trembled through her and she closed her eyes. His arms strained her closer as her tears wet his chest. He lifted her face and rained kisses on her brow, cheek, throat and her own mouth sought blindly for comfort, tasting her salty tears on his lips, tasting the tang of his skin and feeling the hardness of his jaw.

Suddenly without saying a word or looking into his face she pushed herself away from him and ran into the bathroom. Locking both doors, she turned the shower to full pressure and stood under it, letting the water beat against her face. She could never remember a time when she was so weary in body, weary in soul, confused in mind. She clung to the heavy handles of the water controls, half awake, half dreaming, then in an angry gesture she turned off the hot water and for uncountable minutes let the icy cold water cover her, unconsciously punishing herself for her wantonness. Finally she turned off the water and began to rub herself vigorously to get rid of the chill. Wrapping the towel around her she went back into the bedroom somehow knowing Jake wouldn't be there.

Taking fresh underwear from the drawer she returned to sit on the bed. It was then she saw the cup of hot coffee on the bedside table. While she was drinking it she heard Jake in the shower, but her mind was numb from the successive hammer blows which had disturbed it since the night he came back into her life. She stifled a groan as her mind began summoning back, in feverish detail, the events of the night. She had wanted him! She was so disgusted with herself she could scream. She was mad! She was a fool! It had meant nothing to him, she thought bitterly. One more willing woman. Her face burned with self-disgust and she clenched her hands. It had meant nothing to her either! Sex was necessary to him and it had been a way for her to get through the night. She didn't love him, had only thought she loved him at one time. She didn't even like him!

They met in the sitting room almost like strangers. Lindy rinsed the coffee cup at the small sink and up-ended it on the counter. When she turned Jake was holding her coat. They walked down the corridor without exchanging a word and she would have passed the coffee shop if he had not taken her elbow and steered her inside. He seated her at a table and went to the service counter and returned with two plates of food, then eased his long length down in the chair beside her. Lindy looked at the scrambled eggs, the crisp bacon and the buttered toast. Automatically she picked up her fork. She was hungry and finished every last scrap of the food and held out her cup for more coffee.

The coffee shop was crowded and had Lindy been less occupied with her own thoughts she would have been amused at the curious stares and the female interest in Jake. As it was her ears barely registered his voice when he asked if she was ready to leave.

Arriving in the office, Jake told Amos he would need Lindy to help acquaint him with office procedures. Lindy was grateful that he maintained a friendly but impersonal attitude toward her during the day, treating her as a capable colleague. And she had to admit he had a flair for the business — his energy and intuition were truly amazing. When he was working he concentrated with all his attention on what he was doing and yet his fingers flew over the pad making notes, all the time reading, and she wondered how he contrived to do both at the same time.

A kind of brittle calm possessed Lindy. She checked and rechecked details, sorted invoices and performed the million-and-one duties connected with the operation of a large company.

Noon was marked by sandwiches being brought from the coffee shop and the afternoon passed before she was aware of it. Jake worked tirelessly into the evening and she worked beside him, reluctant to break her concentration for fear other thoughts would intrude.

It was past eight when Jake leaned back in his chair. "We've put in a good day's work. Let's go eat."

This time as they walked the corridor they passed the coffee shop and walked on to the restaurant where the lights were dim and soft music played. Lindy had never been here. The decor, the service and the prices were geared to the executive incomes. Jake helped her remove her coat and handed it to the attendant. They followed the waiter to a small candlelit table.

"Shall I order for you?" he asked, then proceeded to do so.

Scarcely ten words had passed between them when they left the restaurant. Her mind slightly dazed by the excellent wine, she stood patiently while he opened the door to their rooms.

"Do you want to use the shower first?"

She didn't answer. She walked into her room and closed the door.

Later when she'd turned out the bedside lamp and slid into bed she pulled the covers up over her naked body and burrowed her head into the pillow. She could hear the sound of Jake's shower over the thunderous heat of her heart. She felt panic and dismay creeping into her mind as she realized what was happening to her. Jake was taking over her life. Her need for him was giving him the power to manipulate her as if she was no more than a wooden doll. It angered her and alarmed her and yet when she remembered the darkness of other nights she began to tremble with fear that he wouldn't come. She stared into the darkness, taut with rage. I hate him, she thought savagely. I hate him for degrading me like this.

The bathroom door opened and he came toward her in the total darkness. He turned back the covers and came confidently into bed beside her. Even as his arms reached for her, she cried out wildly, "I still want a divorce!"

For an answer he caught her close, his mouth searching for hers with fierce, possessive demand, silencing all resistance, forcing hers to open beneath his own. She moaned and fought against the rape of her mouth and tried to push him away. His arms held her in a viselike grip and his naked legs held hers imprisoned between his own. Gasping, she struggled as much against the desire he had awakened in her as she did against the arms that held her. Suddenly her mouth was free.

"Jake! Don't do this to me!" Her voice trembled with the agony she was feeling. He didn't love her, she was a diversion for now and she knew that later she wouldn't have the strength to deny him.

"Hush . . . this is our one line of communication," he muttered unsteadily. "You like for me to touch you here . . . and kiss you here." He stroked the flat stretch of her stomach with his fingertips and trailed his lips down over her breast. "I know you better than you know yourself, sweetheart. You wouldn't let me touch you like this if you didn't love me. If we can share this we can share . . . other things." His tongue made a little circle of her lips. "Don't fight me, darling . . ." he whispered. "I need you. You disturb my nights, haunt my days."

She rolled her head from side to side. "No! It's over! This is all . . ."

"It isn't over!" he grated between clenched teeth and thrust his body deeply into hers.

She raised tear-drenched lashes that scraped against his cheek. "I don't want to love you." She was sobbing helplessly. "I don't have any trust in you so how can I love you?" She evaded his lips. "Even . . . this has no value. It's been offered to so many others!"

Her words made him go rigid for a few seconds.

"Dammit! You're my wife," he almost snarled. "And you'll remain my wife!"

She continued to roll her head in denial. Her eyes were tightly closed though tears still crept between the lids. As if in torment she tightened her arms about his neck and hungrily sought his lips.

"Love me, Jake," she begged as if to shut off the turmoil of thoughts that tormented her.

"I will, sweetheart, and I . . . do," he whispered tenderly in her ear and kissed her so gently that her whole body cried out for him.

Morning came quickly. When she awakened it was to full awareness. She was still cuddled in Jake's arms, her bare legs entwined with his. Suddenly she stiffened and wrenching herself away from him sat up in the bed.

"Oh . . ."

"What is it? What's wrong?"

She was frightened and furious, more at herself than at him, but it was toward him her anger was directed. "What if . . . you've made me pregnant?"

He laughed in relief. "What if I have? Would it be such a crime?" He tried to pull her back down into his arms, but she pushed his hands away.

"I don't want a baby! I've no plans for a baby, ever!" she wailed. "It would be different for you," she accused. "You would continue going from one affair to another and I'd be left to be both mother and father to a child. My child will never live the way I lived, Jake!"

She failed to see the hurt look that came over his face.

"Would you hate having a baby that much?"

"Not a baby. Your baby, Jake." She was cruel and she didn't care.

His hands shot out and grabbed her arms and he shook her. His eyes were cold steel and completely ruthless. He continued to shake her angrily, his eyes moving over her face without compassion. She was almost sobbing with frustration as well as fear of him in this strange, cold mood.

"That's it, isn't it, Lindy?" His eyes glittered strangely. "I'm to suffer because of your unhappy childhood? Because of your father? Grow up! Not all men are cast in the same mold, nor all women. You want to believe the worst of me, don't you?"

"What else can I believe?" She was choking on her rage. "I don't want to talk about it. It's over!"

He was shaking her savagely again, unaware of his anger, of his cruel grip on her arms. "It's not over. Admit it!"

"No! I won't!" She bent her head unable to meet those piercing eyes and his anger suddenly left him. He put his hands on her shoulders and pulled her hard against him.

She quivered in his arms, and he put a hand to her throat and tilted her face up to his. His eyes searched her face as his hand cupped her chin. In spite of herself, she opened her eyes and looked at him. A wave of helplessness came over her, and a little whimper escaped from her lips.

"If you feel so strongly about not wanting to get pregnant, sweetheart, we'll do something about it. But . . . for now . . . let's just take our chances, hmm?"

She kissed him as if he was all that mattered in the world and he drew her back down onto the bed and let his hands roam over her warm skin.

Chapter Four

There was no lack of entertainment at the complex. The oil companies had spared no expense to help their workers fight the stress and boredom of isolation. The self-contained camp offered daily movies, videotape television, saunas and surprisingly decent food in the restaurants. Before many evenings had passed Lindy and Jake had explored them all.

In the weeks since Jake arrived Lindy had lost none of her anxious doubts about the wisdom of what she was doing. But Jake left her no time to sit down and gather her chaotic thoughts and file them in any kind of systematic order. There were so many things to do. Jake completely reconstructed the office procedure; together they made up new weekly, monthly and quarterly report sheets to be sent to the printer. Jake was determined to have a company emblem and they worked long hours on a logo that would be simple, yet instantly recognizable. He left the final design and color up to Lindy and the painting of the logo for the printer to photograph and reproduce took hours of her time.

Lindy allowed one of her rare smiles to

surface when she showed her final design to Jake and Amos. The word "Williamson" in block letters was slanted forward as if bucking the wind and the wind lines above and below the letters gave the impression of a company on the move. The letters were emerald green and set into a red frame that was the outline of the state of Texas.

Jake pinned it to the bulletin board and backed away to look at it. He moved close to Lindy and put an arm around her.

"By God! That's great! You're really good, sweetheart." His hand squeezed her waist.

"It can be made up in various sizes. You can use it on the large equipment as well as the small pieces."

"Will it work on letterheads?" He walked away from her so he could view the design from another angle.

"If it's placed on the side of the sheet with the address and phone numbers across the top for balance."

"Good idea. What do you think, Amos?"

"I like it very much. Lindy would make an excellent commercial artist."

Jake laughed. "Don't be putting ideas in my wife's head, Amos. I need her to look after me and that's a full-time job." He intended to make a joke of it, but a quick glance at Lindy's set face told him he didn't succeed.

Lindy was seldom alone. After work hours Jake never left her side and during the day he conducted much of his business by telephone. In the evenings just before dinner they strolled around the complex. They checked what movies were showing, but seldom sat through one. They visited the disco where the girls went in groups of two or three in hopes of meeting someone interesting. Occasionally they entered a gift shop where the imported items were very expensive. Always they stopped in the solarium to watch the northern lights. It was an awe-inspiring sight. The huge cranes used to unload cargo stood outlined like sentinels in the glow of the flickering lights.

They dined quite late and somehow managed to converse easily. Jake told her about various places he'd visited in South America and she told him about her hope of selling at least one of her needlepoint designs to a national stitchery magazine. Much of their dinner conversation was about the business because Lindy was as knowledgeable about some aspects of it as Jake was. They were both careful not to mention the time they lived together or their reason for parting. Usually by the time they reached their rooms she was rather floating from the effects of the wine she had consumed with dinner and went straight to the shower.

When Jake came to her the room was dark. He would slide into bed and reach for her. She would go into his arms willingly. A few times she thought about the sleeping pills. She missed their tranquilizing effect, but after making love with Jake she could relax and sleep. He was a gentle and patient lover, putting her pleasure foremost before satisfying his own desires. His husky voice whispered love words to her and they echoed on inside her brain.

Only one time did she speak of what was happening between them.

"I don't understand myself! I keep thinking . . . I won't do this!"

"Stop worrying about it." He let the palm of his hand run over her breast until the nipple stood firm. "You like this, don't you?" He moaned silently.

"Yes, but . . ."

"Shh . . . hh . . ." He pressed his mouth to hers each time she started to speak until their hunger grew and there was no time for words.

An air of expectancy hung over the office for several days before the convoy of trucks carrying drilling equipment and replacement parts was due. Jake was impatient for the convoy to get within radio range and called out periodically. Several days after their due date he made contact with the lead truck, via citizens'-band radio, but the transmission was not the best and it was hard to understand the soft Texas drawl coming from the huge eighteen-wheel truck.

"How about it, Buck? You got a copy on this base station?"

"Ten-four, good buddy. I've got you wall to wall and tree-top tall."

"How's things going?"

"Well now, we're a keepin' the rubber side down, but it's been the drizzlin's, good buddy. These eighteen-wheel toboggans has been a slidin' since we left the Yukon." The voice coming in was getting clearer as the convoy got closer to the camp.

"What's your ten-twenty, Buck? Do you know how far out you are?"

"No way of knowin' out here on this white desert, Jake. We'll just keep a comin' till we get there."

"You'll see where to go when you get inside the camp. There's a building about the size of Yankee Stadium where you can drive in and leave the trailers. Whatever you do, Buck, keep the rigs running or the fuel will freeze in this temperature. I'll be down to meet you."

"Ten-four, Jake. I've got a man with a bad back who needs to see a doc. He'll never be able to make the return trip. We'll be a man short."

"We'll figure out something, Buck. Keep 'um rolling. I'll clear with you and head on down to the loading docks. My wife will stand by the radio in case you need to contact us again before you get here. See you in a few. I'm gone." Jake set the microphone down and looked at Lindy. He stared at her for a moment, as if in deep thought.

As he left the office he paused by her desk, took her chin in his hand and gazed at her in a penetrating way. She raised questioning eyes to his and he mouthed the words "You're beautiful." She shook her head trying to free her chin from his hand. He laughed softly as color creeped up her neck to flood her face. She watched him leave and was disgusted with herself for allowing his words to make her blush like a stupid little schoolgirl.

The day passed swiftly. Lindy locked her mind to the work piled on her desk. She wanted to finish so she could leave the office before Jake returned. Betty was excited over the arrival of the convoy and wanted to linger in the office in case the new arrivals came in. She freshened her makeup, ran the comb through her hair and sprayed herself generously with cologne, the fragrance drifting in through the connecting door.

When the outer door opened something deep inside Lindy trembled for a moment.

"Whee . . . ee . . . ee! It sure does smell pretty in here, Jake. Smells like the Rio Grande valley at orange-blossom time."

The man's soft Texas drawl touched off a pang of homesickness in Lindy. She heard Jake introduce him to Betty, heard Betty's breathless attempts to prolong the conversation, as Jake came through the doorway followed by the giant of a man from which the gentle voice had come. Soft, smiling brown eyes looked down at her out of a rugged face creased with smiles. He held a thick wool cap in his hands and the telltale white streak across his upper forehead told her this Texan was more at home in a wide-brimmed Stetson than the wool cap he was twisting around in his large hands.

"This is my wife." Was that pride she heard in Jake's voice? He waited to see Buck's expression, then grinned.

"Well . . . I'll be swan to goodness, ma'am. You sure are pretty! There's no girls prettier than Texas girls no matter where you find 'em and you're one of the prettiest. But tell me, honey, how'd you happened to get caught up by this here old ugly boy?"

Lindy stood up and although she was quite tall she felt dwarfed beside this big Texan. He was so big, so friendly and his manner so much like the truck drivers she had worked with back home that it was impossible not to respond to him.

"Hello, Buck." She extended her hand and it was immediately lost in his.

"Remind me not to ever call you an ignorant, stupid old boy again, Jake."

Jake laughed and slipped an arm about her shoulders. "Believe me, Buck, I know what I've got." He smiled down at Lindy and before she realized what she was doing she smiled back. "We'd like you to join us for dinner," he was saying to Buck. "Wouldn't we, sweetheart?" His hand caressed her shoulder and arm.

"Of course. It will be nice to talk to someone fresh from home."

"I'll be fresh soon as I thaw out. I'll swear it's colder than blue-blazes out there and I been wonderin' what in tarnation this warm-blooded old boy is doin' up here. I'm for giving this country back to the Eskimos!" His eyes twinkled at her. "I'd better go get all slicked up if I'm going to have supper with the boss man and his lady. 'Bye, for now, Lindy." He went to the door. "And 'bye to you, too, little gal," he said to the disappointed Betty.

Jake closed the door between the connecting offices. "You liked him, didn't you?" He said it very carefully. It was the quality of his tone that caused her to look up. He was watching her when she found his eyes.

"Yes. It would be impossible not to."

"Buck affects people like that. He was with me in South America."

The statement required no answer and she went back to her work. When next she looked up Jake sat scowling as though he wanted to kick something. When he caught her glance he leaned back in the chair and tried to grin, but it was not an overwhelming success.

Lindy wore a blue dress that night and Buck gave her the usual chaff about being pretty as a Texas bluebell. She had decided she was going to enjoy this dinner and for her own satisfaction she had done her best to look her best. She looked exquisite — tall and elegant and sexy. She didn't know it but she had a kind of naive glamour about her that caused men to watch her. She had an aura of distant reserve coupled with vulnerability and shyness that made them want to protect her. When they entered the restaurant Jake knew what Lindy didn't, that every man in the room would have given his eyeteeth to go home with her.

Buck was an easy companion and Lindy found herself listening eagerly to him and Jake talk of their experiences in South America. Jake included her in the conversation in a light teasing way that didn't require much of her and allowed her to observe the two men who were so alike and yet so different. When the meal was over and they sat with their coffee Jake took her free hand and held it in his lap, his fingers interlaced with hers.

Three evenings later, after they had dinner with Buck, Jake announced, rather casually, "Get your things packed. We're leaving in the morning."

The calm and mildly spoken words stunned her. Time was meaningless while she stood and stared at him, his words echoing through her sluggish mind.

"What did you say?" Her face was a mask of confusion.

"We're leaving in the morning. We're a

driver short so you and I are going south with the convoy."

"You and Buck knew you were leaving and didn't say a word during dinner! Why?" A pause while she gave him a scornful look. "I'm not going with you, Jake. Who do you think you are to make plans concerning me behind my back?"

"I didn't tell you because I knew how you would react. I was right. Now pack your things if you want to take them with you."

Her eyes were blazing with fury. "I'm not going."

"You're going. I've made sure about that." His eyes, turned green like a stormy sea, seemed to pin her back to the wall.

Dear God, she thought, he means it! Rage struggled with the inner terror that he could make her do whatever he wished. Why did he want her? Why didn't he get out of her life and leave her in peace?

"I . . . you're not . . ." She was sputtering and couldn't help it. Her eyes blazed into his. "I'm not buying this time, Jake. Whatever you're up to . . . I'm not buying." In spite of herself her voice dropped to a hoarse whisper. "I don't . . ."

He cut her off as though she hadn't spoken. "We leave in seven hours," he said, looking at his watch.

"Can't you get it through your head? I'm . . . not . . . going!"

He went on as if he hadn't heard her. "The weather is due to take a bad turn and we want to leave ahead of the storm. Otherwise we wouldn't be in such a hurry. So be a good girl and get packed. I've got a few things to attend to first — I can pack my things in about ten minutes."

Lindy sucked in a breath and tried to keep from shaking. She couldn't take her eyes off his face, feeling the blood drain from hers.

"I don't give a damn about the weather!" The words seemed to explode from tense lips. "I have a job here. I have a room here. I have my life planned, Jake. It doesn't include you."

His laugh was dry and short and not really a laugh at all. "You don't have a job here. You won't have a room here after tonight. Another girl is on the way to take over both your job and your room."

Hating him and herself both, Lindy felt the uncontrollable tears erupt. They gushed into her eyes and swamped her throat. He came to her, caught her shoulders, and she hated him all the more.

"Damn you, Jake!" She was mouthing words, any words. She lifted her head with reluctance, her eyes like two stars between wet lashes and glazed with emotion.

"We're good together, Lindy." He said it very carefully as though he meant it.

She composed herself sufficiently enough to murmur, "Only in bed."

"Thank God for that!" he whispered fervently, and took possession of her mouth, tenderly and eloquent with emotion. When he raised his head he gave a wry smile. "We have our bad moments, but we also have some pretty wonderful ones."

She stood away from him and brushed the thick swath of dark hair back from her forehead. She felt suddenly calm and oddly empty inside. She heard her voice persist. "You're determined to grind me down, aren't you Jake?"

"Not at all. I'm determined to keep you with me, as my wife, my life's partner, mother of my children. I've had two years to think about it, Lindy. I want a home, family, some permanence to my life." Then he made one of his quick moves and caught her shoulders to spin her toward him. His eyes lost that look of warmth and admiration. He looked down at her with cold, interested eyes that narrowed to mere slits and his voice underwent a rapid change, sharp and cruel. "You're not going to flounder around feeling sorry for yourself any longer." His eyes studied her. The determined tone of his voice convinced her she would never be able to hold out against him. There was a moment of fierce glaring between them. Lindy was first to give in.

"Damn you . . . you . . ." Her own tone lacked conviction and was muffled with a kind of pain.

When Jake finally left the apartment and the echoes of his footsteps died away Lindy's first reaction was that of relief. He'd gone and she was alone. With her accustomed self-reliance she tackled the job of packing her belongings. Carefully she packed her completed canvases and then the rest of her things much the same as she did a few weeks ago when she moved to the apartment only this time she left out warm clothing.

Her cases were ready and waiting beside the door before she allowed herself time to think and then her thoughts raced in chaotic confusion. She could not help shivering. The look in Jake's eyes as he had walked away from her made her afraid. Hating him, hating her own weakness for him, her head started whirling dizzily. She lowered it to her knees and hoped the faintness would go away. With defeat in the slump of her shoulders she tried to stand, but she was so dizzy that she held on to the back of the chair while the room stopped swaying. She stood there, her breath quickening, and then a longing almost like a pain washed over her. A longing for the pills that lulled her into unconsciousness and peace.

She walked slowly into the bathroom, catching a glimpse of herself in the full-length mirror as she passed it. It was like seeing someone else. The body was no longer hers. The face, vacant. "You're asking for it . . . you're really asking for it!" It was weird to look at yourself this way and to feel as if you didn't belong to yourself. She wanted to laugh, but laughter would not come. Tiredness welled up in her, enveloping her like a shroud. She passed on into Jake's room and began opening drawers. She felt so lonely, lost and then . . . frantic.

It was only after she searched every drawer, every pocket in the clothes hanging in the closet that she noticed the pigskin bag. Praying it wouldn't be locked she tugged it down from the shelf and dragged it out. With trembling fingers she sprung open the catch. Her hands searched under the neatly folded jogging suit, the knit shirts, the jockey shorts for the round bottle. Disappointment making her want to weep she pulled back the elasticized pocket on the side of the case. Nothing there except two thick white envelopes. Her name, her real name, LuLynn Williamson, jumped up at her. Jake's name was on the other envelope.

Automatically, without will or volition, she opened the envelope with nerveless fingers. The words, the unbelievable words, swam before her eyes.

IN THE DISTRICT COURT OF
THE STATE OF TEXAS
IN RE: THE MARRIAGE OF
LULYNN WILLIAMSON AND
JAKE WILLIAMSON

UPON THE PETITION OF —
LULYNN WILLIAMSON
DISSOLUTION DECREE FILED WITH
CLERK OF COURT
JANUARY . . .

January? January! Her divorce from Jake had become final over a month ago! He had signed the papers without her knowing, the divorce had become final without her knowing. She bent her head. She was free! No longer married to Jake. She crushed the parchment between her fingers. Why hadn't she been told? Why had he pretended they were still married? What a fool she had been to go to bed with him.

She got up suddenly and waited for her head to stop throbbing before she moved toward the bathroom taking the envelope with her. After bolting both doors she stripped off her clothes and got under the shower. The water pounded on her head. She had been crazy, stupid not to take the first plane out of here after he arrived. Why didn't I do it? No one would have stopped me. Don't think . . . relax . . . She held her face to the stinging water, keeping her eyes closed, but her mind kept clicking like a computer. The carefully made plans for her future were not shattered after all. She was once again in charge of her destiny. Oh, God, just one more mountain to climb. She would make it. She had to.

She was hardly aware of the sound of the apartment door closing or Jake's voice calling her name. She was acutely aware, however, of the pounding on the bathroom door.

"So you know." Jake's voice, loud, angry. "It makes not one particle of difference, Lindy. I signed those papers during a weak moment. In fact, after I discovered you were sleeping with Dick Kenfield. It took me a while to realize it was partly my own fault, for going away and that you were lonely. By the time I decided I wanted you anyway it was too late. My lawyer thought he was doing me a favor by rushing it through the courts. We'll be remarried as soon as we get to Fairbanks. Make no mistake about that."

Coming out of her daze she heard his angry words. She hadn't heard right, of course. Either that or she was losing her mind. Dick her lover? Dick could have been her lover. Wanted to be. But, no. She hadn't wanted to have an affair. For the tiniest moment she wished it had been true. Oh God . . . oh, please . . . please don't let me get sucked in again.

Chapter Five

Lindy was alone in the apartment when Buck came for her.

"Will we have time for coffee?"

"Coffee will be waiting for you in the cab." His eyes took in the shadows beneath her eyes put there by hours of sleeplessness. "Jake spent most of the night whipping everyone into shape. We're all lined up and ready to go."

Five minutes later they walked down the long corridor and out into the eerie darkness. It was almost fifty-five degrees below zero and the light from the gas flare made ghosts of the few figures walking on the bleak landscape. The roar of the six huge diesel engines was deafening. A cloud of ice fog floated around each as the drivers revved up the engines. Her appearance was evidently the signal they had been waiting for.

With her overnight case tucked under one arm, Buck firmly clasped his mittened hand around her arm and guided her to the last truck in the convoy. He opened the door and tossed her bag inside. She looked at him with questioning eyes. The step to the huge cab was

94

about waist high. He placed his hands at her waist and as effortlessly as if she were a child lifted her up and onto the seat of the cab. He saluted her with his mittened hand and closed the door.

Lindy had been in truck cabs before and was able to appreciate the luxury of this one. The interior was of soft cream leather and the seats were as comfortable as an easy chair. Between the driver and passenger seats was a compartment for food, complete with a small coffee-maker plugged into the dashboard, and the smell of freshly perked coffee was delicious. It was quiet and warm and had it not been for the turmoil of confusion within her she would have enjoyed the adventure.

The citizens'-band radio came to life. "Break ... break ... break, you Texans. We're headin' home to God's country. The boss man and that little ol' turtledove a ridin' with him will have the back door. We'd better check out these CBs. How about it, turtledove, you got a copy on ol' Buck?"

Lindy's fingers trembled as she grasped the mike and pressed the button. "Ten-four, Buck."

"Did you hear that? Ain't that pretty? We're goin' to be hearing that sweet Southern voice all the way to Texas. Come on, now, you truckin' cowboys, check in so we can get out on the avenue."

As the last man answered, the door opened

and Jake hoisted himself up into the cab. He tore the ski mask from his face and glanced at her. "Morning."

His calm manner irritated her and she granted an answer.

He swung his parka and her case into the compartment behind the cab and picked up the microphone. Holding the mike in his hand he turned to look at her.

"You'd better get out of that coat or you'll get too warm." He set the mike down to assist her.

Lindy accepted his help grudgingly without looking at him.

He spoke into the mike. "We're ready, Buck. Head 'um up and move 'um out."

"Ten-four, good buddy. Take care of that little turtledove. She's mighty pretty."

"Ten-four." Jake turned to her with a half-amused grin on his face. "Turtledove."

"It wasn't my idea," she said tartly.

"Fits, though. You can depend on Buck to come up with something fitting."

He leaned over the wheel and pushed various levers. The big engine rumbled and the truck moved slowly ahead. The headlights sprang on and forged a path into the darkness and Jake coolly maneuvered the big rig out onto the frozen highway.

Lindy stole a glance at his sharply etched profile. Not only was he handsome, but he was strong, capable and . . . ruthless. What a stinking thing it was of him not to tell her about the divorce.

"Wake up and pour some coffee."

She poured a small amount in two cups. Digging deeper into the hamper she found sandwiches, cartons of salad, deviled eggs and a variety of snack foods.

"Anything else?" she asked grudgingly.

"Doughnut." He held out his hand. "Good," he said with his mouth full. "But not as good as the ones we used to get in south Houston. Remember?"

She didn't answer, but she did remember the all-night bakery and the warm chocolate-covered doughnuts. She saw a flicker of humor in his blue eyes as he swung them away from her and concentrated on his driving. The truck picked up speed and she found she didn't want to turn her gaze out the window just yet. Pretending to rest her head back she watched the powerful hands deftly swinging the wheel. There was something terribly attractive about him in a rugged, masculine way, of course, and especially when he was doing the thing he liked best to do. Love or hate . . . it had to be one or the other she felt for him. There was no doubt he suited and aroused her physically, but then, she considered, how do I know another attractive man, Buck for instance, couldn't do the same?

She gave an involuntary shiver at the thought of making love with any other man.

No, dammit! I'm just trying to fool myself. Demoralizing as it is, I love him! It was insane that she could love him after the agony he had put her through. He had no need for the love, enduring love, of a woman. With that arrogant face, the imperious set head and flashing eyes, he could have any woman he wanted. Now that she had admitted to herself she still loved him her lips curled with self-disgust.

"What's the matter?" The strangeness of his voice made her look down at her hands clasped tightly together in her lap.

"Nothing," she said much too reasonably. "I was only thinking."

"About . . . us?"

Suddenly she wanted to cry for all those nights so long ago when she was young and blindly in love. Not being able to define in thoughts or words what she was feeling she turned stricken eyes toward him. "Oh, please, Jake!" Her voice was soft in protest. "This is all so . . . useless."

"Useless?" He echoed the word.

"You know what I mean!" Why couldn't he understand, for chrissake? "We're different people now. I have made a life for myself, just as you have."

He gave a muffled curse and looked across the intervening space between them, his eyes glittering under the lids. "Good God! We're right for each other. Haven't I convinced you yet?" There was a hard, mocking quality to his voice.

"The only thing I'm convinced of, dammit, is that I'm no longer married to you and you didn't even have the decency to tell me!" She stared at him helplessly, also convinced she would never, never be rid of him. Everything about him, his physical attraction, his personality, was making that impossible.

Jake set his mouth in a straight line and concentrated on his driving. The loose snow stirred up by the trucks ahead made for poor visibility at times. It was easy to be bored with the scene. It seemed to go on and on with nothing to break the monotony.

Lindy picked up the road map lying over on the dashboard. Vaguely she wondered about the need for a map. There was only one highway south. But looking at it she couldn't suppress a small thrill at the sight of their journey plotted out across Alaska.

"How long before we reach Happy Valley Camp?"

"It's hard to say." His eyes were on the road. "Buck says it's slow going ahead."

"I didn't get to see any of the country when I came up. We flew from Houston to Anchorage, then on north."

He brought his gaze in from the road. "Actually, I haven't seen much of the country either. Alaska is a very poor and stark region; there are large numbers of animals only because this environment is spread over such a large space. I doubt if we will see many of them."

They were moving slowly now so she sat back and sipped her coffee. Jake, with his eyes on the road, was blindly reaching for his cup. She picked it up and placed it in his hand.

"Tell me about Buck. Have you known him long?"

"Why do you want to know?"

"No reason. He seems nice."

"He is. He was given a rough time by a woman." His voice was hard with cynicism.

She didn't say anything thinking he didn't want to talk about it.

"Buck had it rough," he said again, his voice softer. "He's over it now, but it took a while. His trucking company was about to be taken over by his creditors and I bought it. He had spent every last dime he could get his hands on trying to keep his wife happy. I could have told him it was impossible, but at the time he wouldn't listen to a word against her. She was just plain no good. After a time he came to realize it more than anyone else. Now he can't stand the sight of her."

Lindy settled back in the seat and closed her eyes, trying to relax, but they flew open again as Buck's voice came in from the radio speaker. "Breaker, boss. You and turtledove still back there?"

"Ten-four, Buck. We're about a mile back.

How's the road ahead?"

"That's what I want to tell you. I'm stopping here. Some joker got himself crossways on the road and is being pulled out. We better keep the rigs spaced in case the traffic on this boulevard gets heavy. If he don't treat you right, turtledove, you just come on up here and ride with ol' Buck."

Amusement, curiosity and surprise all mingled in Jake's eyes as he looked at her. "Forget it, Buck." He hung up the mike.

He pulled the heavy truck over to the side of the road. After pulling several levers and adjusting gears he leaned back and flexed his arms over his head. Turning sideways in his seat he reached for the coffee.

"Tired . . . turtledove?" His tone was a mixture of ridicule and teasing.

"Don't call me that ridiculous name!" Her face suddenly showed the agony of last night and he watched her, puzzled by the torment he saw mixed with fatigue. He took her hand and stroked it lovingly, holding it tightly when she would have jerked it away.

"Give in, Lindy. Don't torment yourself. Our marriage can be a good one if you'll give it a chance."

Lindy was sitting up very straight, looking at him defiantly from beneath half-closed lids, her hand cold and taut in his. She forced her lids open although they felt as if a lead weight was attached to each one. His face was grave and his eyes held a tenderness she didn't expect.

"We are worlds apart, Jake. Oh, I admit the marriage would be good from your standpoint. A little woman waiting at home, one that is good in bed, a loving, trusting, dumb little wife who would take care of the babies and go to PTA. That scene is not for me. I'm simply not interested. I prefer a man who doesn't lie and cheat. When I'm with you, Jake, I'm treading on quicksand. There's no feeling of stability. I prefer a straightforward life with a straightforward man to match."

He tilted his head and took in a deep breath of air into his lungs. His face was a dark mask and there was harshness in his voice.

"Someday . . . someday you'll push me too far and I'll take a strap to your butt!" His eyes flickered over her face, the firm classical lines, the perfect contours, the flawless skin. A movement in his throat betrayed the fact that he was swallowing his anger. He looked dangerous, his steely eyes sweeping across her face, lingering on the pulse that beat so frantically at the base of her throat. "Life can't be played out like a romantic novel with all the characters neatly conforming to what's expected of them. How dull to have each event of the day marked out all prim and proper! You can't deny the pleasure you feel when I hold you against me. Don't try and tell me our lovemaking isn't as pleasurable for you as it is for me."

"That's all you think about." She flung him a tormented look. "That's all I am to you, a body! You don't want a wife — you want a live-in mistress."

"Shut-up!"

Jake's eyes were suddenly so furious that she felt as if the strength drained out of her, leaving her limp in the grip of the hands that clutched her forearms.

"You look like a woman, but you're really a child, Lindy." His dark face was adamant as he looked at her, the lean jaw set and firm. "You're welcome to hate me, if you really do. Frankly I know you love me and you'll marry me again when the time comes." He slid a panel aside and folded down a section at the back of the seat which made a step up to the door behind. "Get on back there and rest. You look like you've been run on a rim for five miles."

Lindy gazed back into his eyes, so astonishingly green and luminous in the dim light. "I'll never live with you," she said distinctly. "It would make me ill to have to see you day and night for the rest of my life. Haven't you got it into your arrogant head, Jake, that I despise everything about you, the look of you, the sound of you and especially the touch of you? I'm free and nothing . . . I mean nothing, would cause me to marry you again."

He flinched when she said that and if it were

possible went a little pale under the sun-tanned skin. His facial bones seemed to stand out with additional clarity and the pupils of his eyes expanded and darkened. He looked as if she had kicked him in the throat.

Lindy felt a thrust of pleasure that she had actually bruised his pride and climbed into the back compartment and slid the panel shut with force.

She lay down on the bunk, pulled the blanket up over her and gave herself up to the flood of misery that engulfed her. Her torment was all the more difficult to bear because there was no one with whom she could share it. She longed to be home where she could talk with her friend, Debra. Calm, practical, reliable Debra whose own marriage ran like the romantic novel Jake scoffed at.

Lindy's troubled mind was unable to separate fact from fantasy, now. Built-up emotions of the last few weeks found release in the silent sobs that shook her thin body. All at once tiredness attacked her with an odd sense of detachment and she slept, her tears making a damp pillow under her cheek. She awoke once, conscious of the moving motion of the truck, but was lulled again into the sweet oblivion of sleep, where her mind need not strain to work out the problems that confronted her.

Sometime later the unfamiliar stillness of the truck awakened her. The only sound she heard was the soft purr of the motor which she knew would not be turned off until they reached warmer climate.

She was wide awake immediately, tense and alert. Raising her head from the pillow she saw the covered figure on the narrow pull-down bunk opposite her. His back was toward her and the blanket was drawn up to his ears. She sank back down into the warm nest of blankets trying hard to resent his being there. Her face touched soft fur and she recognized Jake's fur-lined parka. He must have placed it over her while she slept. By the feeble light she checked her watch. She had slept hours and it had seemed only minutes. She settled herself down to wait out the remaining hours until morning. Unconsciously she drew the fur collar under her face and snuggled her nose into it. Strangely the masculine smell was comforting. She felt safe, contented, and fell into a tranquilizing inertness, then into deep peaceful slumber.

Chapter Six

Lindy awakened to the sound of buzzing and her sleep drugged mind thought it was made by hundreds of bees. Full consciousness came to her and she opened her eyes to see Jake sitting on the other bunk, using a battery-powered shaver. He was rubbing the instrument over his face and his eyes were on her. She looked into the blue depth and saw the twinkle of amusement there. His mood had changed, but hers hadn't. She glared back at him.

"Good morning."

"Good for what?" she replied shrewishly.

"I can think of a number of things and so could you if you weren't feeling so sorry for yourself!"

She clamped her mouth shut and tried to look away from him, but in the closeness of the compartment there was no other place to look. He seemed to fill the tiny space. She wished desperately that she wasn't lying down.

He read her thoughts and lifted his brows in a way that made her want to strike out at him. "When I finish shaving I'm going to kiss you," he said, trying to keep his mouth from spreading in a wide grin as her eyes opened wide and her mouth set stubbornly. He was shaving under his chin and tilted his head back, but his twinkling eyes never left her face.

"You're hopeless, Jake. A real imbecile!"

"Yeah?" He turned off the shaver. "But you love me."

"You're not only an imbecile, you're conceited!" In her agitation she sat straight up on the bunk.

He laughed aloud, produced a comb from somewhere and ran it through his hair. "You're even more attractive when you're mad. I don't remember you getting mad in the old days."

"The old days are over!" she almost shouted at him. "This is now!" That reminder of the past tore at her heart.

"Yeah." He said it softly and took her chin tightly in his hand. She tried to twist away from him, but he held her firmly and ran the comb through the tangles of her hair.

She strived to close her heart against the thrill of his warm fingers on her face and the gentle look in his half-closed eyes. His magnetism seemed to draw the anger out of her.

He tucked the comb into his shirt pocket then brought his hand up to smooth down the hair that fit her head like a cap. His fingers lingered on her ear, then slid to the nape of her neck. The thumb of the hand holding her chin rubbed gently back and forth across her tightly compressed lips. Suddenly he laughed.

"The first time I kissed you your lips were just like this . . . shut tight!" His laughing eyes searched hers. "But you soon opened them . . . you liked my kisses, remember?"

Her eyes glittered. "I didn't know what kind of an idiot you were then."

"But you know now," he said softly, laughingly, "and you still like them."

She shook her head in denial, knowing that he knew she was lying.

"Shall I prove it?" With her head in the powerful grip of his two hands she was helpless as he slowly lowered his lips onto hers. He kissed her with slow deliberation, his lips playing, coaxing. He had kissed her many times before with passion and urgency, but never did she have to fight so hard not to surrender completely. He caressed her gently, almost delicately, encouraging her by his very control to lose hers utterly. Oh, sweet Jesus! She had to hold out against him. She had lost so much already!

His hands left her head and slipped down her back, pulling her tight against him. She felt herself sliding down on the bunk until she could slide no further and the pressure of his body on hers made every nerve and sense in her body suddenly vibrantly alive.

"You . . . beautiful, tantalizing little witch!"

His shaking voice said into her ear, "Tell me you don't love me, if you can."

Her eyes were haunted and dark with despair when she looked at him. "I never said I didn't love you. I said I didn't like you and that I won't . . ."

"Hush," he said quickly. "I don't want to hear what you won't do!"

"No . . . no!" She tried to push him away. "I must be out of my mind! Get away from me, Jake! Get away from me!" Resentment burned like wild fire. With blinding clarity the truth hit her like a tangible blow. He realized his power over her!

He got up and sat on the opposite bunk and ran his hand through his hair. "You're warped."

"I may be warped, Jake, but I'm not stupid. Marriage to me didn't keep you from taking another woman and you've had other women since you left me . . . deny it, if you can."

"You know I can't! What did you expect me to do?" The tender look was gone from his eyes and his voice was fringed with sarcasm. "Dick Kenfield and then Amos and you dare to criticize me!"

"I wish I had slept with every man that asked me!" Her sarcasm matched his.

He got to his feet and stood towering above her, glaring down at her as if he hated her.

"I would have killed you!" he snarled. Snatching his sweater from the bunk he went through the door of the compartment. Once again they had parted in anger.

Lindy lay on the bunk staring at the closed door. Peaks and valleys, heaven and hell. It would always be like this with Jake.

The last twenty-four hours seemed to set the pattern for the days ahead. The convoy furrowed its way south across snow-packed plateaus, one-way bridges, detoured past overturned rigs and slid down icy mountain sides. The atmosphere inside the truck cab was comparable to the conditions outside. One moment smooth going of an easy comradeship, the next stormy battles of will against will.

They passed through Atigun Pass and on south to Old Man Camp settlement, crossed over the first permanent bridge over the mighty Yukon River, stood by on the siding while dozens of dependable rigs passed heading north with their loads of long pipe — the most sophisticated ever designed to meet the requirements of the rugged terrain. After Five Mile Camp the road was considerably better and knowing the next stop would be Fairbanks and hot showers, good beds and a few days of rest the men settled down to the job of getting there in the shortest time possible.

"Won't be long now." Jake grinned at her.

"I'm going to sit in a hot tub and soak away all my aches and pains."

Looking straight down the road, his next

words were spoken matter-of-factly, belying their importance.

"We'll be married again in Fairbanks."

He hadn't mentioned the marriage since the first stormy quarrel they had shortly after they left the camp and Lindy was about to think he had given up on the idea of a quick ceremony.

She tightened her lips and looked straight ahead, resentment in every line of her face.

"Now don't start balking again," he said sternly, and then trying to joke her out of her sulky mood, he added, "I think I'll start calling you Muley."

"Call me anything you like, but you're a fool if you think I'm going to jump back into the frying pan!"

"Dammit! I don't know why I bother with you!"

Lindy's chin lifted, her own pride fighting to control the pain inside her. She turned her face away and looked out the side window at nothing in particular.

"Break! Break!" Buck's voice came in on the radio. "Number two's jackknifed. It's still upright, but a-sittin' on the side of the ditch."

Jake slowed the truck and at the same time picked up the microphone.

"Ten-four. John, you and Charlie go on ahead of Buck. Don, you stay on this side of the wreck and I'll pull up behind you."

Jake turned on the flashing emergency

lights and steered the heavy truck as far as he dared to the side of the road. Pulling on his parka he glanced at Lindy's set profile, muttered a muffled curse and got out of the cab slamming the door behind him.

Lindy watched Jake lope down the highway and out of sight beyond the truck ahead. Her tense body relaxed and she slumped against the seat. This was the first time in two days she had been alone and no longer needed to keep up the pretense of the self-assurance she had assumed since the start of the trip. Not wanting to think about the problems she would face in Fairbanks she looked out the window trying to find something that would catch her interest. There was just a lot of ice and snow, occasionally a small hill, or a drift.

She could see nothing of what was going on up ahead and was tempted to get out and walk just for the exercise and to break the boredom of waiting. A northbound truck stopped ahead and suddenly, she had a powerful urge to see for herself what was happening. Something was wrong, she could feel it. Her heart started to pound swiftly and she reached into the compartment for her parka and boots.

When she was ready to face the biting cold she crawled over into the driver's seat and let herself out of the cab holding onto the door until her feet could feel the firmly packed snow. Up ahead she could see the men running back and forth in a frenzy of activity. Spotlights were being focused on the truck which had slid down the incline and was lying precariously on its side.

Lindy stood hesitantly in the shelter of one of the truck cabs, the roar of the big engine drowning out the voices of the men. Try as she might she couldn't spot Jake. It was Buck's bulky figure at the top of the bank shouting instructions to the men. Where was Jake? She ran across the snow and grabbed Buck by the arm.

"What's happened?"

"What are you doing here? Didn't Jake tell you to stay in the cab?" They were the sharpest words she ever heard him speak and for a moment she was taken aback. Then it came to her . . . something had happened to Jake!

"Where's Jake? What's happened?"

Buck looked down into eyes wide with anxiety. "Jake went around the trailer to attach a cable and it slipped over on him."

Lindy's face went white, she caught her breath and felt the sandwich she had eaten an hour before rise up in her throat.

"Can't . . . you get him out?"

"We're trying, honey. We've got an emergency call out for help. That's all we can do for now."

"Is he . . . hurt . . . bad?"

"We don't know. That's the God's truth!" Anguish was in every line of Buck's face as he stared down at the bedlam in hers.

"Do something! We can't wait!" Her voice was rising to an almost hysterical pitch and she started toward the overturned truck.

Buck grabbed her arm. "Stay back!" he said sternly. "We can't risk it slipping more."

She stopped in her tracks sure that she was going to fall apart. Jake couldn't be . . . gone. He would come climbing up over the bank and be mad because she was out in the cold. He wouldn't leave her now! He had sworn . . . had promised he was never going away again! Oh, God! She couldn't face all those nights alone again! Why didn't he come up from behind that truck, dammit? He was just doing this to teach her a lesson! Jake, damn you!

One of the men was talking to Buck. "If we had a way to get a chain through that small hole and get it hooked onto the undercarriage we could use the winch to lift it enough for one of us to drag him out. If he is alive he won't last long as cold as it is."

"It's a good idea, Don, but there's no way in the world we can get a chain under that truck. The hole is just too damn small."

Don looked at Lindy. She looked back and suddenly read his thoughts.

"How big is the hole?"

Don made a circle with his hands, but still said nothing.

"I can get through a hole that size, Buck. I can do it!"

Buck looked at her as if she had lost her mind. He shook his head and glared at Don before bringing his eyes back to Lindy's anguished face.

"If Jake's alive it's because the truck hasn't settled and it could do that any minute. If that happens he won't have a chance and neither would you if you were under it."

"I can do it, Buck! You've got to give him a chance! Let me do it! Please!" The determined ring in her voice and set to her shoulders caused Don to grin.

Buck looked down at her for a long moment before sudden hope flared in his eyes, then died slowly.

"If anything happened to you Jake would kill me."

"He won't be here to do anything, for chrissake, if you don't make up your mind!" There was something agonizing in her eyes that tore him.

"You understand if that truck slips it will crush you like a melon?"

"Just tell me what to do." She felt as though someone else was speaking the words for her. She heard them, but couldn't feel them in her mouth. There was an incredible numbness that settled on her like a giant cloak.

They walked to the truck and knelt down in the snow to peer into the hole. Suddenly everything was functioning; her mind, her body. Her manner was of total control; it was only her eyes that shouted her anguish. She shrugged out of her coat. Someone handed her a toboggan cap and she pulled it down over her head.

Buck put a chain with a giant hook in her mittened hand and explained what she was to do.

"Straight through the hole and to the right you'll see a big round steel loop on the under-side of the frame. Put the hoop in the eye from underneath so when we pull up the strain will be on the outside of the hook, understand?" She nodded. "Now, honey, I don't know what you'll find when you get under there. Get the hook fastened as fast as you can and we'll pull you out." She nodded again and lay flat on the snow. Buck tied a rope to one of her ankles. "Yank on the rope and we'll pull you out," he said but she barely heard him.

Lindy inched her way carefully into the small hole. There wasn't much room for maneuvering the big chain, so she dragged it along with the big hook looped into the belt of her jeans. She didn't dare use her elbows to push herself forward, so she clawed with her fingers and the toes of her boots. The blood was racing through her veins now and her heart pumped madly, but her mind was clear and her nerves steady. It took several minutes of crawling before she could see Jake lying at the end of the small tunnel. She kept her eyes fixed on his face trying to see some sign of life.

Oh, God! Please let him be all right . . . she wanted to tell him she was sorry for her bitchiness . . . that she loved him . . . that at this moment she would forgive him anything.

The eyebeam where she was to attach the hook was ahead. Her eyes once again sought Jake's face. His head was lying in blood-soaked snow and his leg was twisted and out of sight beneath the frame. She had to force herself to move away from him.

Lifting the hook from her belt she slipped it securely into the hole and pulled on the rope to let Buck know she was ready to come out. As she was pulled backward she kept her eyes on Jake for as long as she could see him. Fear tightened her throat at the sight of him lying there so pale and defenseless.

Don untied the rope from her ankle, helped her into her parka and enveloped her in a blanket. She had started to shake uncontrollably. Buck shouted orders and the men hurried about preparing to lift the machine.

"We'll have only seconds," Buck was saying. "I'll shout when I get to the other side. Start the winch slowly. When it's clear enough I'll drag him out. The frame will buckle. Let's pray to God it don't buckle before I get him."

Don and one of the other drivers stood beside Lindy. "Good girl," one of them said. "At least he's got a chance. I hope Lady Luck's ridin' with Buck. He's gonna have to move fast."

Lindy stood as if in a trance while the winch

tightened the chain. She knew only one thing. Jake was under those thousands of pounds of steel, and she might not ever see him alive again, might not feel him, touch him, argue with him. He had broken his promise to her, had slept with other women, had been unfaithful to their marriage vows . . . but what did that matter now? Tears ran down her face like summer rain. Dammit, Jake! Don't you dare die on me! Cold to the heart she watched the heavy chain tighten, heard the groan of the straining winch. Her glance shifted to Buck poised beside the end of the trailer.

Suddenly he darted out of sight and the group on the road held their breath. Seconds later he was dragging Jake's limp body out and down the ditch. He had only just cleared the wreck when the metal began to twist and the trailer buckled, settling heavily on down the steep grade. It was all so quiet. Like a silent movie. Even the men who ran to help Buck bring Jake up the bank didn't speak.

Gently they placed him on folded blankets and covered him with several more. Lindy knelt down beside him.

"He's alive! Thanks to Lindy, he's alive!"

"We've got to stop the blood!" Lindy was losing control.

"The ambulance is almost here. I can see the flashing lights. We called for it on the emergency channel as soon as the truck turned over on him." Buck put his arm around her.

"You were great, honey, just great. If he lives he'll owe his life to you."

"Don't say that!" Her anxious eyes watched the still face on the ground. Oh, God! she felt so helpless.

Buck pressed a cloth to the wound on Jake's head, trying to stem the flow of blood that ran down his face which had taken on a gray tinge. Time hung like a black cloud while they waited for the attendants to come with the stretcher. Fast and experienced, they made every move count and within seconds of their arrival Jake was in the ambulance.

Lindy and Buck stood outside the door of the emergency vehicle while the skilled rescue team worked over Jake. Lindy could never remember any of this with clarity; she was conscious only of the heavy dread around her heart and the weakness of her limbs. The tension mounted as the team continued to work. Just when she thought she couldn't stand the suspense a minute longer the door opened and one of the attendants called out.

"Does anyone know this man's blood type?"

Buck shook his head, but Lindy came to life. "Yes, yes! It's the same as mine!"

"You're sure?" The attendant looked at her closely. "It may save his life if we can give him a transfusion."

"We gave blood to the Red Cross two years ago. Our blood type is the same." She was shaking violently and Buck held her arm.

"Are you his wife?"

"Yes," she said without hesitation.

"Come on then!" He pulled her into the ambulance and almost before she got inside the door he was taking off her coat. "Lay down." He briskly pressed her to the cot beside the one where Jake lay.

While preparing the instruments for the transfusion the doctor questioned her about any recent illnesses. She told him she had not been ill.

"Good." He injected the needle into her arm.

In seconds she could see the tube between her arm and Jake's filling with her blood. The strain and the tension were taking its toll on her and she felt giddy. Closing her eyes she willed herself to stay conscious. She wanted desperately to question the doctor and stared up into his face trying to read his reactions.

"We're going now." The doctor's voice was quiet, unhurried. "Any message for the men?"

"Ask Buck to come to the hospital." For the first time since the accident she was conscious of the large tears in her eyes.

The siren started, the ambulance moved, the doctor sat between her and Jake, his watchful eyes on the needles in their arms.

A little color had come back into Jake's face by the time they reached the hospital; weak tears streamed down Lindy's when they were separated. Jake was taken to the emergency room and Lindy to a small office where she was given orange juice and a few crackers which she forced herself to eat. The weakness in her legs made her realize she needed the food. While she was resting she gave the registrar as much information as she could about Jake. Married? She had to say no. Age? Thirty-three. Service record? Vietnam. Next of kin? Her heart almost stopped at that question. It seemed hours before she was allowed to leave the room to wait in the small anteroom reserved for relatives of patients in emergency. She rested her head against the wall and closed her eyes wearily.

Chapter Seven

Lindy reached for a magazine and let her eyes wander over the pages hardly reading what she saw. She was filled with apprehension, her heart fluttering, her fingers trembling as she turned the pages. Was no one ever coming to the little room? Her ear was tuned . . . listening for footsteps. Waiting was agonizing. She threw the magazine down onto the table and went to the door. The long hall was empty except for a white-coated orderly pushing a cart at the far end. She was surprised at the lack of activity, then remembered it must be terribly late at night. The long day had turned into a nightmare. On almost uncontrollable legs she went back into the room and sank down on the sofa, covering her eyes with her hands.

Footsteps were coming along the corridor. Her heart lurched. Dear Lord, let it be good news!

Buck's big frame filled the doorway. His face looked tired and drawn, his eyes searched her eyes, asking the question. "Any news?"

She shook her head despairingly. "No. No one has come at all."

Buck looked down at the tired pale face. Her dark-circled eyes were dulled with fatigue. She still wore the clothes she had worn when she crawled under the truck. She had gone through quite a lot today, both mentally and emotionally. She had also suffered physically, but she was holding up pretty well.

"Had anything to eat?"

"A little," she said wearily. "I could use coffee, but I was afraid to leave in case someone came with news."

"There's a dispenser around the corner. I'll be right back."

Lindy sank down in the chair, refusing to give way before the tears that wanted to spill over again. How desperately she had wanted someone to come! It would be easier now, sharing the waiting with Buck.

He brought coffee for the two of them. Lindy accepted hers with a bleak smile of thanks.

"It seems like I've been waiting forever, Buck." Her voice was tired, old. She swallowed something in her throat, something that felt like a large lump of cotton that wanted to rise up and choke her.

"I came as soon as I could, honey. I stayed only long enough to hire a couple guys to take my rig and Jake's on south. The men are at the terminal now loading the cargo. Don will handle things and I'll stay here with you."

"Thank you," she said, took a deep breath

and felt as though things would never be right again.

"Why don't you lie down on the couch and rest?" Buck suggested.

"I couldn't. Oh, Buck, I've done so many stupid, childish things! I don't know what I want anymore!"

By way of answer, Buck held her hand tightly. They didn't talk, but they were mentally in tune with another. Buck cared for Jake too.

Lindy tensed at the sound of voices in the hallway. She rose like one compelled by a force many times stronger than herself and faced the door. It was as if her whole being was about to dissolve as she waited for someone to appear.

A tall gray-haired man entered the room. "I'm Doctor Casey."

"Yes?" She was breathless.

"Mrs. Williamson?"

"Yes."

Buck was on his feet, extending his hand. "Buck Collson."

"The blood given to Mr. Williamson at the scene of the accident saved his life," the doctor said after he shook hands with Buck. "He has several injuries, but what concerns us the most is the head injury. We don't know the extent of the damage. We had to remove a small piece of his skull to relieve the pressure from an optic nerve. He must be kept absolutely quiet for the next twenty-four to thirty-six hours." He quietly studied Lindy for a moment. "You told the emergency doctor he was your husband and the registrar he wasn't married."

"We're divorced," Lindy said quietly.

"I see. Well, he's fretting about something and calling for you. It may calm him to hear your voice, but I wanted to see you first. You must not allow any of your anxiety to be transmitted to him. He must not be upset. I cannot stress that too strongly."

The doctor was regarding her keenly, assessing her. Lindy looked straight into his eyes. "I can do whatever has to be done, Doctor." Her voice was calm, steady, even to her own ears. But, oh, God! If he only knew how she wanted to cry.

"Good. Come with me."

Lindy hesitated and reached for Buck's hand. The doctor nodded his permission for Buck to come and they followed him out of the room and down the hallway. The long white corridors seemed endless and Lindy was glad of Buck's reassuring fingers beneath her elbow.

When they reached the door of Jake's room the doctor paused and looked at Lindy's calm, composed face once again, then opened the door for her to pass through.

The room was of generous proportions with wide windows and light green walls. The dark-clad figure of the sister nurse stood on one side of the bed, a white-coated orderly on the other, his hands holding the shoulders of the man thrashing about.

Lindy's eyes were drawn immediately to Jake's tanned face. His head was swathed in bandages that came down over his eyes and was held firmly in position by supports placed on either side. The part of his face that remained visible was unrecognizable to her. His mustache had been shaved, the cuts around his nose and mouth stitched, long scratches extended from his jaw to his neck. Restless hands moved back and forth over the white sheet and periodically he tried to lift his shoulders only to be gently pressed down by the strong hands of the orderly. Protruding out from under the sheet that covered him was a leg, encased in a cast, resting in a sling suspended on the foot of the bed.

She stood there for a long moment, afraid to go in, but knowing she had to. Then slowly, one foot after the other, she walked into the room and stopped again. Her brain started to resume its normal function. The murmured words of the man on the bed reached her ears.

"Lindy . . . Lindy . . ." The words came from puffed lips in a hoarse whisper.

The sister stepped aside and made room for her beside the bed. She came close and took his long, slim hand in both of hers. The swollen lips parted and he breathed out words that only she understood.

"Lindy . . . believe me . . ."

Tears coursed down her cheeks and fell onto her hands that clasped his. The hand that had always been so strong and capable was weak and clung to hers. She leaned her head so her lips were close to his ear.

"I believe you, Jake darling. I believe you and I love you. Please lie still. You must lie still and rest . . . sleep, darling." She whispered into his ear and touched her lips gently to his cheek.

The hand in hers trembled slightly and then clutched hers with a strength that surprised her. She brought it to her cheek and spoke to him softly and soothingly.

"Go to sleep. I'll be here. Everything's going to be all right."

He murmured something once again. She bent over him talking softly, reassuringly, scarcely aware the orderly and the nurse had gone to the end of the room to speak in low tones to Buck and the doctor.

Someone placed a chair behind her and she sat down close to the bed. The hand in hers was still holding hers tightly but the restless movement of the other hand had stopped as had the movement of the shoulders. Lindy looked askance at the doctor, who nodded to her, and motioned Buck and the orderly toward the door. He followed them out after giving instructions to the nurse who seated herself at the end of the room.

Jake's breathing was more even now, as if he were sleeping. The fingers holding hers gradually loosened their hold and lay passive in her hand. All at once she felt herself trembling uncontrollably. The shock and surprise of seeing him so helpless, vulnerable, was just now catching up with her. She held the limp hand tightly. He had called for her. Could it mean that he loved her? Really loved her after all? She sat gazing at his face and gradually her nerves calmed. An inner strength exerted itself and she put all thoughts of the future from her mind. All that was important, now, was Jake's complete recovery.

The minutes and the hours ticked away. She was silent and motionless, her eyes never leaving the bruised face. She didn't let herself wonder why his eyes were bandaged. For now it was enough that he was alive. The fact that he wanted her, needed her, and she was able to comfort him was soothing to her troubled mind. The traumatic experiences of the long day were taking their toll on her strength. She leaned over and rested her cheek on Jake's hand where it lay on the bed. Her eyes drifted shut and she slept.

She awakened gradually, her drugged senses resisting consciousness. When full awareness came to her she was lying on a bed, a light cover over her. Buck was sitting in a nearby chair, his head resting on his arm. He appeared to be sleeping. Lindy sat up and threw off the covers, her thoughts flying to Jake.

"Buck!" Her wildly frightened heart pounded.

Buck got quickly to his feet. "He's sleeping, honey-child. Rest while you can." He came to her. "The nurse will let us know if there's any change."

She sank wearily back onto the bed. "Oh, Lord, Buck. What would I do without you?"

"You'd manage, honey. You got starch in that backbone."

She smiled weakly. "It only appears to be so, Buck. I'm really scared spitless."

"Yeah, I know. Me too." He was tired. It showed in the lines in his face and the bleak expression in his eyes. "I've checked us into a hotel. After a while we can go shower and change clothes. That'll make us feel a hundred percent better."

"What time is it?"

He smiled wearily. "It's morning. Can't you smell the breakfast being carted down the hall?"

"As late as that?"

"Rest a while longer. I'll go see what I can find out."

Later, while luxuriating in a warm, scented bath, Lindy let her mind mull over the information Buck brought back from the doctor. Jake's condition had stabilized and he was sleeping, which was what the doctor wanted him to do. Buck had broken the rest of the news to her gently. The doctor feared Jake's eyesight was going to be affected by the blow he had received on the head. He said he wouldn't know for several days the extent of the damage. He also suggested the possibility that the nerve would repair itself and Jake's eyesight would return to normal. It would require long and patient care and he would need to be kept quiet and relaxed. The joy Lindy felt that he would live was replaced by a cold dread of him being unable to see. How would he handle it . . . how could a vigorous, active man like Jake accept blindness, even for a while?

The hotel was a new modern structure that fairly screamed the word "expensive" when they walked in the door. Lindy had been hesitant but Buck propelled her toward the desk and demanded their keys with all the confidence of a Texas millionaire. On the way to their rooms he had assured her the company could afford the expense.

"Old Jake would have my hide if I put you up in anything less than the best." Buck's drawl and humor was coming back.

The room had been far more luxurious than anything Lindy had stayed in before and under different circumstances it would have been a delight to sink into the big tub and sprawl out onto the giant bed. She wanted to linger in the warm tub, soaking her tired body, but she hurried through her bath and was ready and waiting when Buck rapped on her door.

Buck was a good-looking man. Several feminine heads turned to look at him as they passed through the lobby. He was wearing a Western suit that had been tailored for his large frame. His raven hair was shiny as if he had just come from the shower. The ever-present cowboy boots and sheepskin coat flung over his arm fairly shouted this man was from Texas. Why couldn't I have fallen in love with a man like Buck, Lindy thought. He's gentle, thoughtful, comfortable to be with. He's so different from Jake who constantly sets my blood to racing and my heart to pounding.

She was too tired to notice what Buck ordered for her to eat, but when the waiter set the bowl of steaming soup in front of her, she realized she was hungry.

"You know about Jake and me two years ago?"

He was watching her and she found his eyes. "Jake told me."

"Tell me about him. About what he's been doing the last two years." She hesitated. Damn! She wanted to know and she didn't want to know. Her eyes picked out a spot past Buck and she gazed at it intently. "I've wondered . . ."

Buck drained his cup and set it aside carefully. "I've known Jake for a long time. Even before you came into his life. It wasn't until after you two split that I got to know him well and to find out what a really fine person he is."

The waiter refilled the coffee cups.

"I ran into him one day in Houston. He had just got back from South America and was going back again. The fact that I was about to lose my company was common knowledge and Jake asked me, right out, if I needed help. He offered either a loan or to purchase the company, leaving me in charge." Buck's fingers twisted around his cup. "You know the answer to that. He bought the company. But more than that, he stood by me through a messy divorce and helped me get my personal life straightened out. He went off to South America and left me on my own, saving my pride before my men. I had to produce; I couldn't let him down."

Lindy wasn't surprised by the story. It was something Jake would do. She was surprised that he would have the money for such an investment.

"He made several trips back to the States," Buck said taking up the threads of his story. "He'd stay a few days and be off again. I went back with him about a year ago. We came back to Houston a few months back and Jake set out to buy the Prudhoe Bay company." He grinned. "I couldn't understand at first why he had to have that particular company." Looking away from her he continued. "Jake's a very shrewd business man. Dead wells he leased years ago are now pumping close to eight hundred barrels a day. Financially he's pretty well set. Once he starts the ball rolling he usually gets what he wants. But you should know that. Before he left Texas he bought a house on Galveston Island and left exacting instructions on how it was to be furnished. He set a time limit of one month for the work to be finished." Buck looked at her searchingly. "He came north to get you, girl, and take you back to that house on the island."

Lindy felt as if her heart had turned over inside her. She wondered if, in fact, the loud thump of her heart could be heard all over the room and she had an almost uncontrollable urge to cry. Biting her lip hard, she looked at Buck with agony behind her eyes, making them look large and bleak.

"We planned to have a house on the island one day." The words were whispered and her lips trembled. "And we window-shopped for furnishings." Now . . . why did she have to remember that?

"Didn't he tell you about the house?"

"No. He never even told me about the divorce being final. I happened to find the papers in his suitcase."

Buck smiled at that. "He was mad as hell at himself for signing those papers and fit to be tied when we came back and the divorce was final."

"I'd made up my mind not to marry him again and I was going to leave him when we got to Fairbanks, but now . . ."

"And now?"

"And now I don't know. I couldn't leave him like this in spite of . . ."

"In spite of what?" he urged.

"In spite of the fact I'd be standing in hot water if I marry him again!" she blurted. "I'd never know from one day to the next if he . . ."

"If he what?" Buck persisted.

"If he was out with another woman! I'm old-fashioned, Buck. I want to be the only woman in my husband's life."

Buck sat back in the chair, lit a cigarette and regarded her with thoughtful eyes. He marveled at her self-control. Her voice was steady and direct when she spoke again.

"Women gather around him like flies wherever he goes. I was told by someone who knew him very well that no one woman would ever satisfy him and I believe it. I know what it means, Buck, to live in a home where there's love only on one side, where the laws of religion keep a couple together until death do they part. I'll never raise a child in that atmosphere. If I marry Jake again it will mean I will never have children!" Tears came to her eyes. "And more than anything I would love to have a child of my own."

Buck's dark brows drew together. "Honey, I don't know what to say. Guess I never gave no thought to that side of it. One thing I do know, Jake's a proud man. It would be a bitter pill for him to swallow to be accused and have his wife refuse to believe in him."

So he did know the reason for the separation. She wanted to cry. It seemed to be all she did anymore. So much had happened. It was all so crazy sitting here talking to practically a stranger, but she had to get it out.

"But what about me, Buck? What about me?" The question seemed to be wrung from her tortured heart.

He shook his head. He longed to reassure her, but the words he chose seemed so terribly inadequate.

"You'll have to decide if you love him enough to take him as he is. One of you will always give more than the other. Accept it or you'll end up hating each other like my former wife and myself."

Chapter Eight

Lindy spent every possible moment with Jake, moving from his bed to the corridor to his bed and back to the corridor. Buck joined her on this treadmill for there was no getting her away from the hospital except for short periods of sleep. Although Jake was kept heavily sedated and fed intravenously, he seemed less restless when she was there.

One time she thought him awake. He gripped her hand tightly and said in a clear audible voice, "My love . . . my life . . ."

Poignant tears sprang quickly to her eyes. He had whispered the familiar words many times while making passionate love to her, holding his ardor in check, infinitely patient, waiting to take her with him in the final floating away.

She gazed at the bruised face. He was sleeping. She leaned over and placed a feather of a kiss on the swollen lips. She felt afraid suddenly, as if by his very helplessness he was binding her closer to him.

Forty-eight hours after the accident the doctor intercepted Lindy and Buck on their way to Jake's room and invited them into his office.

"Mr. Williamson is conscious and alert this morning. I don't think it wise for you to see him for a few hours. I prefer we give him time to adjust to what we have told him. Oh, yes, we told him the absolute truth — the fact that we are not sure he will be able to see when we remove the bandages and also that we have every hope his eyesight will return." The doctor paused and looked at Lindy. "He was concerned about your reaction to his temporary blindness, Mrs. Williamson."

"What do you mean?"

"I got the impression he wasn't sure that you'd stay with him," the doctor said bluntly and looked away as if not liking to say these things to her.

"I won't leave, now. That is if he wants me to stay."

"I suggest you tell him that." Doctor Casey's voice was kind. "It's important to his peace of mind. He will recover much faster without mental stress of any kind."

Buck spoke up. "How long will this temporary blindness last?"

"We have no way of knowing how long it will take for the nerve ends to heal, but I will say this . . . if his sight hasn't returned within six months, his condition will have to be reassessed and the decision made at that time on further treatment. He'll be able to get around in a few days. We'll put a walker on the bottom of the cast on his leg and he can move about. Well, that is about all I can tell you for now. Come back this afternoon. We're going to remove the bandages now and Mr. Williamson will rest for a few hours. I'll assure him you will be back." The doctor smiled. "Mr. Williamson is a very lucky man."

"Lucky?" Lindy echoed.

"Why yes. I understand you and his friend risked your lives to get him out from under the overturned machine. Another few minutes and he would have bled to death. You also gave him blood and will stand by him during what is going to be, for him, the most traumatic few months of his life. I would say he's very lucky."

Lindy looked from the doctor to Buck feeling that the doors were being firmly shut behind her and there was no way out.

Later that afternoon Lindy paused at the door to Jake's room and clutched Buck's hand.

"I'm scared!" Her voice was barely audible.

"Relax, honey, and play it by ear. That's all you can do." Was there ever a man so calm and reassuring? "I'll wait and see him later."

Bracing herself, as if to do battle, she opened the door, slipped inside and closed it softly. Hesitant steps took her toward the bed, her eyes going immediately to Jake's face.

The large bulky bandage she had become used to seeing had been removed and in its place was a smaller one that covered the upper part of his forehead and extended into the hairline. A pair of dark glasses, more like blinders than glasses, covered his eyes. His face had lost its puffiness and except for the pallor under his tan he looked much better than when she saw him last. Her eyes never left his face as she went toward him, her heels making small tapping sounds on the tile floor. He was covered with a sheet that reached only to his bare chest and his arms were lying at his sides, his fingers spread out and pressing against the bed. She could tell by the tilt of his head that he was alert and listening.

"Lindy?" He raised his hand toward her.

She put her hand in his and he gripped it so tightly she winced, but kept the pain out of her voice as she spoke to him. "How did you know it was me?"

"Your perfume. Have you always worn the scent I gave you?" His voice was surprisingly strong.

"Always." Her eyes misted over.

He brought her hand up to his face and rubbed the back of it against his cheek. She had to strive hard to keep from sniffing back the tears.

He seemed to relax a little and a slight smile hovered around his lips. "Do I rate a kiss?"

"Several." She bent over him and placed light kisses on his face and laid a gentle one on his mouth.

"That's not the kind of kisses I want," he complained.

"That's the kind you're going to get until the cuts around your nose and mouth are healed and the stitches out."

"Do you plan to be around when they're healed?" The question was asked tensely, abruptly. She was startled by the question and the tone of voice.

"What do you mean by that? Do you want me to leave?"

His answer came promptly. "You know damn well I don't! Well . . . are you?"

"Of course I'm not going to leave if you want me to stay." Her voice was low and vibrated almost angrily.

He lay very still. Finally he released her hand and his fingers moved up her arm. "You're still standing. Is there a chair nearby?"

"Yes. I'll get it."

She sat down close to the bed and let her fingertips touch his arm so he would know she was near. He made no attempt to reach for her hand so she moved it away.

"I want us to marry again," he said bluntly. "I've been thinking about it all day."

She watched him for a moment and said nothing. He was like a caged hawk. "All right."

He didn't move, but lay with his head turned toward her.

"All right? But it isn't what you want, is it?" He spit the words out bitterly.

She was shaken because suddenly it was what she wanted. "Yes, darling. It's what I want."

"Darling?" He echoed her words for the second time. "Quite a . . . switch." An unyielding look settled on his face. "Well, never mind that now. The doctor said Buck was with you. He'll help you to make the arrangements. Where is he?"

Lindy swallowed hard before she answered. "He's waiting outside. Shall I call him?"

"Not just yet. Tell me about the accident."

Not knowing how to deal with his sudden change of mood she tried desperately to keep the tremor from her voice.

"I don't know much about it, Jake. Buck will be able to tell you all the details. The convoy left two days ago. Buck stayed here to be with you."

"With me or you?"

Lindy drew her breath in sharply. The cynical question hurt her and she tried to keep it from her face, then remembered he couldn't see. "To be with you, of course." Now what was he thinking?

There was a short silence.

"I'll need help, there's no doubt about that!" His fingers formed a fist and pounded on the bed.

"Yes, you'll need help." She said it more sharply than she intended. "We'll see if you're man enough to accept it graciously."

To her surprise, he laughed. It wasn't a real laugh, more like a grunt. "I'm man enough to accept help, little cat, but not pity. Not from you or anyone. Understand?"

"Perfectly, Jake." She felt cool, calm.

Uneasy silence hung heavy between them. Jake clasped his hands together across his chest and turned his head as if looking away from her. She was confused. She had said she would marry him. She had been going to say she loved him, but his aloofness had hit her like a dash of cold water. What thoughts could be going through that handsome head? What had caused him to turn so cold and remote all of a sudden?

"Jake? Why can't we wait until we get back to Houston to remarry?" She reached over and placed her hand on his clasped ones and was encouraged when his fingers captured hers. He turned toward her, his voice hard.

"What's the matter? You getting cold feet about marrying a man that can't see?"

"Don't say that!" She got to her feet. "Your blindness is temporary. Doctor Casey is sure of it."

"And if it isn't?"

"It is! Won't you ever change, Jake? You're being a stubborn fool!"

His face was so pale. Oh, Jesus! Why did she have to argue with him? The doctor said no stress and here she was lousing up everything.

"Trying to figure out a way to back out, my love?" He said it with a sneer that cut into her like a knife.

"I won't back out, Jake." He made a contemptuous, dismissive sound. "I'll leave you and send Buck in. I don't know if I'll be back tonight . . ."

He interrupted her with a sharp, "Why not? Got another date?"

"No," she answered equally as sharp and thought, oh, darling, don't be such a grouch! "A good-sized blizzard is going on outside. The taxi that brought us here may not be able to bring us again."

His body was still except for the faint rise and fall of his chest. He was quiet for a moment, then held out his hand. She placed hers in it and he pulled her closer.

"Bend down."

She leaned over and his hand found its way to the nape of her neck and he drew her lips down to his. He kissed her soundly. She knew the effort hurt him for when she raised her head she could see beads of perspiration on the part of his forehead not under bandages and he let his arm fall weakly to the bed.

"Get Buck," he said hoarsely.

Through a mist of tears she made her way to the door and paused to look back before she opened it. His face had gone so white she took an instinctive step toward him and drew in a great gulping breath to steady herself.

"Is there anything I can do for you before I go?" She made no attempt to disguise the concern in her voice.

"No. Nothing." The coldness of his tone was unbearable and somewhere deep in her heart a small hope died a quiet death.

She walked slowly down the hall. Somehow she felt humiliated and dreadful doubts assailed her. She paused at the drinking fountain, and as she drew a cup of water a quote came to mind, "Humiliation must be borne with head held high." Oh, darn! Let some other jerk hold his head high. She wanted to tuck hers under her arm and cry.

"How did it go?" Buck asked when she reached the waiting room.

"He wants us to be married again right away." Her voice was not ringing with joy.

He smiled warmly and kissed her cheek. How dare he be happy when she was so miserable?

"I'm glad, honey. You'll make it go this time."

"He's not in a good mood so . . . be patient with him."

"Sure, honey. You can count on it. I know Jake pretty well. He's an independent, ornery cuss, and this will be hard on him, but he'll hack it with our help."

"That's just it, Buck. We must not help too much."

"Smart girl. You're right, of course."

"I'll wait for you here," she called to him as

he retraced her steps up the hall.

Sinking down on the couch she leaned her head back and closed her eyes and tried to imagine what it would be like to be blind. Total darkness . . . for weeks, months, a lifetime!

Her eyes sprang open. "No!" she said aloud and began pacing back and forth across the small room. She tried to drive the cold dread from her heart by remembering Doctor Casey's reassuring words, "No permanent damage, however . . ." Damn that "however"!

Buck's visit with Jake lasted much longer than Lindy's. When he finally came from the room he suggested they have a light dinner in the hospital coffee shop. He looked more sober than he had an hour ago. She saw him watching her as she watched him. He held her long in the grasp of his eyes.

"Well . . . how is he?"

"His physical condition is far better than I expected considering what he's been through, but . . ." He paused. "He's bitter, inconsiderate. It isn't like him to be so cynical, so hard-nosed about what he wants."

"He's facing all those months of darkness, Buck. He can't help but feel frightened and bitter. We'll have to overlook a lot."

They sat silently while the waiter served their food and when they were alone again Buck pulled an envelope from his pocket. He studied it for a moment and returned it to his pocket.

He chuckled. "His mind runs like a computer. I had to make notes. He wants to see you before you leave the hospital."

"He needs to rest. Do you think I should?"

"Yes, honey. Humor him. He told me exactly what he wanted me to do. Number one, take you to dinner and see that you ate well because your voice was weak and he thought you were tired. Number two, bring you back to his room while I check the weather. Number three, I was to give him the weather report and he would decide if you were to go back to the hotel or spend the night here."

"You've got to be kidding me!"

"He was dead serious. His mind is sharp as a tack and he's taking nothing for granted."

Lindy's eyes grew large as bewilderment spread across her face. "You mean he is that concerned about me?"

"Concerned isn't the word I'd use."

Quick tears sprang to her eyes. "I can take care of myself and him, too, if he would let me."

"Go along with him. Keep him happy and free from worry as best you can. And love him. A man needs love."

His wistful tone caused her to glance at him. It wouldn't be hard to love him. Not hard at all.

"A woman needs love even more, Buck."

He left her at the door of Jake's room. She tapped lightly. After a brief hesitation she reached for the knob only to have the door open suddenly and a sister, in black habit, blocked the doorway.

"Tell her to wait, nurse." Jake's voice reached into the hall.

When the door had closed she leaned her forehead against the cool wall of the hallway. The harshness in his voice cut into her like a whiplash. Buck was right when he said Jake was inconsiderate.

She was so busy with her thoughts the time flew. The door opened and the nurse came out carrying a tray. She indicated with a nod of her head that she could go in.

Jake was lying much the same as when she left him, but he had removed the dark glasses. For a moment her heart leaped with the hope he could see. His head was turned toward her. She looked into his eyes and caught her breath. How odd that they could appear just the same, only expressionless. Her gaze shifted to his hands and the spread-out fingers pressing down on the bed.

An almost overpowering feeling of love for him came over her, a feeling of protectiveness, such as a mother would feel for a helpless child. A chair had been placed close to the bed and she went to it. Taking the hand he lifted in both of hers, she held it to her cheek before her lips moved across the knuckles, made white by the tight grip he had on her hand. Neither had made a sound, but a great sigh left his lips and she could feel him relax as she continued to hold his hand to her face.

Presently his fingertips loosened themselves from hers and sought her cheek. His dark lashes shuttered his blue eyes and a half smile came to his lips.

"Talk to me, sweetheart." His fingers traveled over her face, caressing her cheek and chin.

"About what?"

"Just talk. Tell me what you're wearing." The blue eyes were open and he had turned toward her. His hand reached out to caress her hair and his eyes closed wearily.

Trying hard to keep the lump from her throat she deliberately made her voice light. "I'm wearing the tan sweater I wore the night we made the Texas chili."

His hand left her hair and traveled down over her shoulder and across her breast and came to rest at the slender curve of her waist. His forefinger forged its way into the tight waistband of her skirt.

"And . . . ?"

"A heavy wool skirt and knee-high boots. The skirt is flared and has huge square pockets."

"A skirt? I haven't seen you in a skirt since . . ." His voice trailed away. "But if it's blizzarding why didn't you wear snow pants? Or did you want to look nice for Buck? It couldn't have been for me! You knew I couldn't see you!" His voice was unmistakably harsh and his nostrils flared angrily.

Lindy couldn't believe that he was angry. In seconds his mood had completely reversed. "Why would you say a thing like that? I . . ."

"Don't bother to explain!"

He removed his hand from her waist and laced his fingers together across his chest. He turned his head straight ahead as if looking at the picture hanging on the wall. It was then she saw the soiled spots on the bedclothes. A tiny line appeared between her eyes and she chided herself for not understanding. He had not wanted her to see him dribbling his food!

She leaned over him and gently kissed his tightly compressed lips. He remained impassive and her eyes grew dark with hurt, but being determined to make things right again she laid her head on his chest. She could hear the rhythmic beating of his heart and after a while his hand came up to smooth back her hair and fondle her ear. Again she could feel the tenseness go out of him. They remained thus until they heard a soft knocking on the door.

Buck came in and stood at the foot of the bed.

"The storm is over," he announced. "They got a snowplow out there as big as a Texas bulldozer, Jake. You just never saw the like. They plow that snow up into a row in the middle of the street and another machine comes along and scoops it up into trucks that haul it away. It's the darndest sight you ever saw."

"Maybe I'll see it sometime," Jake said, his face rigid. "Did you find out anything?"

"Yup, I sure did." Buck took the envelope from his pocket and scanned the scribbled side. "The chaplain here at the hospital will call on you. There's a chapel here where the ceremony can be performed. As for the blood test required for the license, yours has already been taken and Lindy can stop at the emergency room on her way out. The technician on duty will take her blood sample. We'll apply for the license in the morning and the wedding can take place day after tomorrow if Doctor Casey approves."

"He'll approve." Jake had a cold sardonic smile on his face. He lifted his hand to Lindy. Dazed by the rapidity of the arrangements she put her hand in his and he held it tightly.

"Tomorrow buy a white wedding dress. Buck will give you the money."

"Why should I buy a white dress? I'm a married woman! Remember?"

He chuckled dryly and turned his head toward Buck. "She didn't used to be so difficult, Buck. It takes some getting used to." To Lindy he said, "Buy something pretty."

She didn't answer at once.

"Lindy?" His voice reached her again.

"Yes, Jake. I'll buy a pretty dress." She stood numbly looking down at him, all her assertiveness gone. "I think we should leave now. You've had a tiring day."

"Yes, I have. See that she gets safely back to the hotel, Buck."

"You can depend on it, old man. I'll wait outside, honey."

"Honey?" Jake said as soon as the door closed behind Buck. "What else does he call you? Sweetheart? Darling?"

"Stop it!" She had thought he couldn't shock her any more, that she was attuned to his moods. She was wrong. "What's the matter with you? Good Lord, Buck is your best friend. For him it's just a matter of speech. He doesn't even realize it."

"Doesn't he?" he said dryly. "Well, never mind. Were you going to kiss me good night without me having to ask you?"

"Yeah. Hello, good-bye and all that stuff in between and you don't have to ask me, you . . . turkey!"

She kissed him tenderly, sweetly, trying to avoid the stitched places on his face that might give him pain. She tried to be gentle, but he resisted her attempt with his hand behind her head and held her to him.

"I don't want you to go," he whispered. "Stay with me. Stretch out here on the bed beside me." He breathed the words into her ear.

"You're insane. Do you know that?" She bit him gently on the neck and raised her head. "I'll be back in the morning."

"Buy your dress first so you can tell me about it." His voice was polite, almost casual.

Hurt again she nodded, then remembering he couldn't see, said, "All right, if that's what you want."

He held onto her hand until she started to move away from him, then let his fall to the bed. She went quickly from the room.

Buck was waiting outside the door and they walked silently down the hall.

Chapter Nine

Lindy sat alone in her hotel room. She and Jake had been married that afternoon in the hospital chapel. It was beyond her understanding why he had insisted on making a production out of this ceremony. Their first nuptials were spoken before a justice at City Hall and were just as binding as this one.

Jake had been standing and waiting for her when she came down the short aisle on Buck's arm. When she took his hand it was cold and trembling and she knew he was making a supreme effort to stand erect. The red scar lines around his mouth and nose showed vividly on his cleanly shaven face. It was one of the few times Lindy had seen him in a dark suit. She had chosen a light blue wool dress and matching pumps. The ensemble was simple in design, but well suited to her slender figure. She had resisted the saleswoman's attempt to sell her a matching hat.

During the ceremony Jake slipped the ring she had worn once before back on her finger and seemed to be surprised when she slipped one on his. She had bought the ring, on impulse, the day before. At the proper time he kissed her deeply. She was careful not to cling to him. Still in a state of shock, still stunned by the enormity of what she was doing, she stood firmly beside him being as supportive as he would allow.

Doctor Casey, who with Buck was witness to their marriage, gently urged Jake back into the chair that had wheeled him to the chapel. He sank into it wearily as he had used up much of his strength getting ready for the wedding and standing during the ceremony. Lindy followed him back to his room where, at his insistence, a reception, of sorts, would be held.

Standing beside his chair she could tell by the lines around his mouth that he was very tired, but when she spoke to him he smiled and held out his hand to her. They were served champagne along with the tall wedding cake complete with miniature bride and groom on the top. It was beautifully decorated and Lindy described it to Jake in detail. Adhering to tradition she cut the cake and placed the first bite in his mouth. The cake as well as the champagne would be served to the hospital staff and those patients whose conditions would allow it.

It all seemed so unreal to Lindy. She hadn't got used to not being married to Jake and here they were going through a ceremony that seemed to be totally unnecessary. She left the room when the orderly came to undress Jake and get him back into bed. He was exhausted and almost asleep when she returned.

"God . . . I'm tired. This is a hell of a wedding night for you, babe."

"It isn't as if I'm a blushing bride." For once he didn't argue; he was too tired to do anything but just lie there.

For a moment she felt a wave of pity rush over her. Why did she feel so protective of him? Why did she have the feeling he couldn't cope with his blindness without her? Was it because for the first time since she had known him he was in the position of needing someone? For this short while she had all his attention, could hold him, take care of him. It wouldn't last. There would be awful times ahead; terrible times full of hurt and humiliation. He would disappoint her again and again and a little of her would die each time.

Looking down at him, as he slept there like a very tired little boy, she knew she was going to lose in the end. It was insane to look at one's own ultimate heartbreak so calmly. There was a brief flash of bitterness as she thought of her mother and wondered if there ever was a time when she looked down on her father with this inner feeling of resignation.

In her hotel room, Lindy fingered the one rose she saved from her bouquet. Three dozen white roses here in the frozen north must have cost the earth. It had been a very emotional day. Less than two weeks after discovering she was free of Jake she had married him again. Her mind was a little numb, but she had set her course for better or worse and with that thought in mind, she went to bed.

When she left the hotel room the next morning she intended to take a taxi to the hospital, but decided to walk instead. After a huge breakfast she needed the exercise. The air was crisp and she breathed deeply. The sidewalks had been cleared. In places the snow was piled so high she couldn't see over the top. This was a new experience for her and she walked briskly, being careful not to slip on the icy spots. Several small birds hopped ahead of her on the walk and she wondered how they managed to survive the blizzard. Cars passed her with a foot of snow on their tops, snow tires allowing them to move in the soft snow. Children, bundled in snowsuits, played in the snow. It all seemed very normal.

She was greeted by staff members as she walked down the hospital corridor. Her friendly but quiet, unassuming ways had made her popular with the nurses as well as the aides and orderlies. Before reaching Jake's room her hand went automatically to smooth her hair, forgetting, once again, that he couldn't see her. She stood hesitantly in the doorway. Jake was talking on the telephone.

"The oil stock, Mark. Yes, all of it. I want

her to have some security if anything happens to me. Hold on, Mark." He covered the mouthpiece with his hand. "Sit down, sweetheart. I know that's you hovering in the doorway. I heard you coming down the hall. I'm talking to Houston."

"Let me wait outside, Jake."

"No. Come here to me. I'll be just a minute more." He held out his hand and waited until she put hers in it. "Here again, Mark. Take care of that for me right away. Buck will be getting in touch with you. I was thinking of sending him on back down there, but Liz is such a wonder. She'll keep things running slicker than clockwork until I get there. God, I don't know what I'd do without her right now." He squeezed Lindy's hand. "Lindy and I will be coming back soon." Another pause. "Thank you, Mark. Yes. Yes, she's very beautiful. That's the hardest part of this . . . not being able to see her. Yes, all right. 'Bye." He handed the telephone to Lindy and she returned it to the table beside the bed.

"Come kiss me, Mrs. Williamson." He was sitting almost upright in the tilted bed. "Sit here." He patted the bed beside him.

His arms reached for her when he felt her weight on the bed, then clasped her to him, his lips hungrily seeking hers. A terrifying sweetness swept through her veins, sending her pulses and her blood racing. Jake, too, was trembling. When he finally took his lips from hers, his voice shook as he said, "I dreamed of this last night. This . . . and other things."

"What other things?" She would have pulled back from him, but his arms refused to let her go.

"Like you being here so I could do this . . . and this . . ." His voice was a soft whisper and his hands moved beneath her sweater and roamed over her bare skin and into the lacy cup that held her breast. "You smell so good and your skin is smooth and soft and you don't seem to have any bones," he said softly. "Have you always gone limp and trembly when I've kissed you like this, and touched you, like this?"

"Always."

"Then I think you should know that I'm about to drag you into bed with me," he murmured and his mouth kissed every part of her face.

This was the Jake she had fallen in love with, the gentle coaxing lover. She knew there was much more to him than this and that loving him meant accepting the whole man. Her love for him seemed to well up and overflow.

"Jake . . . someone might come in." Her protest was weak, her words fading as his mouth moved to cover hers. His kisses were sweet, giving, tender in their urgency, and then as if beyond his control, hard, possessive and demanding. He was breathing heavily and broke the kiss to allow his lips to move to her cheek where he murmured so softly she almost lost the words.

"You love me. I know you love me."

He held her quietly for a moment and stroked her hair. When he released her she sat up and looked at him. His face was different this morning. No longer tense, scowling. His lips twitched because he knew she was looking at him. She couldn't resist placing one last kiss there.

"You'd better get away from me, woman, before I have you between the sheets."

"And risk having the sister catch us?" She laughed. "Oh, no!"

"It might be worth it! But . . . I suppose I'll just have to wait till we get to the hotel. Now sit still. I want to tell you about our new house on Galveston Island."

Watching the expressions flit across his face Lindy thought about his almost unconscious arrogance, but his enthusiasm disarmed her and she found herself softening as she watched him.

"It's down the coast a couple of miles . . . a nice area. You'll like it. The house faces the gulf and has a covered deck going around three sides of it. Not much grass yet, but quite a few palm trees. The beach is fine white sand, not too many people go out there. It's nice and private. Just the kind of house we talked about having." He reached with uncanny aim for her chin and squeezed it gently. "I ordered furniture before I left, but if there's anything you don't like you can send it back."

"How many rooms?" A woman's curiosity coming forward.

"I don't know, sweetheart. I didn't count them. I do know that there are several bedrooms. I'm going to board them up . . . all but one. I don't want any company for years and years!"

"Stop teasing, turkey. I was thinking about the kitchen." Her tone was heavy with indignation.

"I was thinking about the bedroom in general and the bed in particular." His tone mocked hers.

"Sexy man!"

"You better believe it! What else?"

"And an egotistical, insolent libertine!"

As she ended the words he pulled her firmly back into his arms. He held her tightly for a while then swatted her behind.

"I forgot to tell you, there's an apartment above the garage, which by the way is large enough for three cars and a boat."

"Three cars and a boat?" she echoed. "My . . . my . . . You've come up in the world, Mr. Williamson."

"I didn't say we had them, dumb-dumb. But . . . we could if we wanted to. The oil leases I bought up the year before we were married have paid off. You could say we're loaded, Mrs. Williamson."

"You mean to tell me that I've got to start putting on the dog? Have teas? Crook my little finger and all that stuff?" She tried to sound pained, but her tone lacked conviction.

"Be as uppity as you want, Mrs. Astor. But not with me. I'll spank your royal butt!" His hand slid around and under her hip and he pinched her.

"Masher!" She could hardly keep her eyes from his face.

"Hush and listen. A Mexican couple live in the apartment. I've known Carlos for years. He hasn't been married very long, but his wife, Maria, is a fabulous cook. They'll be a big help."

Lindy was silent for a long while before she said, "I don't want help in the house, Jake. I like to cook. What will I do all day?"

He laughed a clear boyish laugh. "Guess!" His lips hovered over hers. "You'll be taking care of me! Anyhow, Mrs. Williamson, I have to leave the country every once in a while. Carlos and Maria will take care of the place while we're gone." He paused, the kiss he intended for her lips landed on her nose. "You'll go with me until our baby comes. You may have to stay at home then . . . for a while."

Lindy lay still in his arms as a tinge of fear swept through her. No baby! No baby . . . ever! He can make all the decisions but that one. I relied on this man once before and it almost killed me when he let me down. I grew up . . . fast. Nothing lasts forever. As wonderful as this is right now I can't count on it lasting. And I know better than anyone the price a child pays living in an insecure home.

Jake touched her cheek. "What's the matter?" His hand moved down over her shoulder and over her breast. "Why is your heart beating so fast? Does it excite you to think about us making a baby together?"

She was trembling. "We won't start a family right away."

"Not right this minute, but I'd like to." He whispered the words between kisses.

"But . . . Jake." He was so intoxicating, so seductive.

Not allowing her to talk he kissed her again, his mouth burning hers. She responded to his kiss, and yet a terrible ache tugged at her heart.

Disengaging herself from his arms, she moved away from the bed and sat in the chair. Her eyes were clouded with worry, but she didn't allow her apprehension to show in her voice.

"I love my ring. I didn't realize how much I'd missed it."

"Would you rather have a larger diamond?" he asked quietly.

"No!" she stated definitely. "I'm not the type for large, flashy diamonds."

He stretched out a hand to her. She met it with hers. His fingers touched the ring. "You won't take it off?"

The question was strange and she looked at him sharply. It seemed his eyes were looking down at the hand he was holding.

"No. I won't take it off," she promised.

His head on the pillow rolled wearily away from her. She hadn't realized he had been so tense waiting for her answer. Then he said another strange thing that was to linger in her mind. It was simply, "Thank you."

She was touched by the humble remark. New hope began an elusive dance through her thoughts. Deliberately she stilled those thoughts, closed her eyes and emptied her mind. When she looked at him again he lay still, his eyes shuttered.

"Would you like me to go so you can rest?"

"No. Of course I don't want you to go." His voice was curt, his eyes springing open. "I'm getting up this afternoon. I've got to get my strength back so we can go home."

The telephone rang and she asked, "Shall I answer it?"

"Please."

"Is this Jake Williamson's room?" a soft Southern voice asked.

"Yes." Lindy's heart began to pound frighteningly.

"May I speak to him?"

She placed the phone in Jake's hand. "I'll wait outside."

"No. Stay here!" The words were spoken softly, but the tone was a gentle command.

He waited until the tapping of her heels on the tile floor told him she had returned to the chair beside the bed before he put the phone to his ear.

"Hello." After a moment, he smiled. "I'm getting along fine." Another pause followed with a short laugh. "Don't worry, Liz. I'm fine. Hey, don't worry. I'll have Buck call and give you a full report. Will that make you feel better?" Pause . . . "That's my girl. Now, tell me about the Allied contract." He listened while Lindy stared at his bruised face. "Yeah? Of course I knew you would. Thanks, honey. I'll make it up to you. Yeah? Losing my sight is damned inconvenient, but with your help, love, I'll get by."

Blood drained from Lindy's face and the fear she had felt since the phone rang materialized into a sickening knot in her stomach. She thought she would surely be sick. It couldn't be starting again so soon! Liz! She was evidently more to him than an employee, Lindy thought miserably.

"Liz . . ." Jake's voice reached her through the ringing in her ears. "Lindy and I will be coming home soon." His hand reached out to Lindy and for the first time since his blindness she ignored it. "Yes." He let his hand fall to the bed. "Yes, she's changed during the last two years. We both have. Her change is for the better. I know how to pick my women. Didn't I pick you? Thanks, love. I'll tell her.

'Bye for now. I'll call you tomorrow. And, Liz, remember what I said about not worrying. Yes, well . . . 'bye."

Jake held out the phone. Lindy took it and hung it in the stand. A thought went winging wildly through her mind: Liz and Jake! She was consumed with jealousy. Jake appeared to look straight at her. The silence which stretched between them was taut, like a wire stretched to breaking point. Tensely she waited for him to speak while her own muscles ached with the effort to keep still. She wanted to speak, to ask him why he had come back into her life, but the words would not form themselves. She realized with a quiver of guilt that she was glad he couldn't see her, glad he couldn't see the misery she was feeling.

Jake leaned back, a faint smile curving his mouth, yet she had the impression of a wariness about him as if he were waiting for some reaction from her.

"You like Liz, don't you?" he asked softly.

Had he been able to guess her thoughts while she stood there? Guilt made her quiver again and she said quickly, trying to stifle it, "She's not important enough for me to either like or dislike her."

"She is to me." Under slanting brows his eyes did not seem blind between narrowed lids. She stepped back a pace.

"Your business," she said with a nervous laugh. "I want to give the flowers some fresh water." Her heels against the floor made rapid clatter as she left the room.

Holding her breath for fear Jake would call her back she hurried down the hall, the water in the vase spilling onto her sweater in her haste. She reached the door of the public restrooms in time to avoid meeting Buck who was coming toward her down the hall. She darted into the sanctuary and leaned against the wall with her eyes tightly closed. A wave of self-pity engulfed her. What had she let herself in for? How could she have been so stupid? A man like Jake never changes. He had even used his temporary blindness to get what he wanted.

She pushed herself away from the wall and emptied the water from the jar. She refilled it and jammed the roses into the vase. They were hateful to her, as if they represented something tarnished and false. The stricken eyes that looked back at her from the mirror on the wall were large and bright with unshed tears. She couldn't weep. Her misery struck deeper than tears could wash away. She gazed at herself and as she did so a cold hard shell of indifference settled over her. Did she love Jake or only need him as a buffer against loneliness? For a few minutes she thought she was crazy . . . then things began to clarify in her mind.

Debra had insisted once that she attend an assertiveness training session. What was it that the instructor had said? "Lack of action and indecision increase your feeling of helplessness." She came to a decision and breathed a sigh of relief at having made up her mind. Hell . . . she was a person with her own fundamental worth. If Jake was such a shallow person he constantly had to build up his ego with extramarital affairs that was his hang-up, not hers. Her obligation to Jake would be over when his sight returned. She would stay with him until that time. She owed him that.

She went back down the hall carrying the vase carefully now.

"Hello, Buck." She set the vase in the same spot from which she had so hastily removed it only a short while ago.

"Hello, honey. Been watering the garden?"

"Expensive flowers take a lot of water." She picked up her purse. "I'm going to lunch."

"To lunch? After all those flapjacks this morning?" Buck's voice was laughing, but his eyes were not.

"Suddenly I'm hungry. I'll see you later, Jake."

Going down the hall she was quite proud of herself. None of the pain, sorrow, loneliness, disillusionment she was feeling showed in her face.

She killed several hours in the downtown area. She bought a novel for herself and several magazines and newspapers. In a new and up-to-date needlework shop she examined commercially painted needlepoint canvases with a critical eye and compared them to her hand-painted originals. She was pleased with the comparison. Her one-of-a-kind canvases would find a market in Houston where needlework-conscious women would appreciate their quality.

Reluctantly she hailed a taxi to take her back to the hospital for her afternoon visit with Jake. She wanted to hurry and get it over with so she could go back to the hotel, have a hot bath and perhaps work for a while on her own needlework. Her visit to Jake had become a duty, an obligation, and nothing more.

Chapter Ten

The door to Jake's room was open when she reached it. She was surprised to find him sitting in a chair by the window, a blue robe over his pajamas and his broken leg propped up on a footstool.

"Lindy?"

"Yes. It's me."

"I thought those were your footsteps coming down the hall."

"Yes," she said again. "My heels are quite noisy. I should have rubber put on."

"I like to hear them."

"I brought the *Dallas Herald*, the *Des Moines Register* and the *Chicago Tribune*. I couldn't find a Houston paper. I think they must sell out fast with so many Texans in Alaska. I also brought a hunting magazine. Shall I read to you?"

"Not just yet." He said it tensely. "Why did you leave so suddenly this morning?"

"Suddenly?" She laughed. "I was here for several hours."

"You know what I mean, dammit. You know damn well what I mean." His face was turning red and his hands gripped the arms of the chair.

"I'm afraid I don't, Jake. Now, do you want me to read to you or not?" She ignored his angry tone and deliberately made her voice conversational. He could take his damned arrogance and shove it! Did he expect her to be all sunshine and light after listening to him seducing Liz over the phone?

"I sure as hell don't want you to read to me until you tell me where you've been for the last four hours." There was a low vibrancy to his voice, an indication he was keeping a tight rein on his anger.

"You mean I'm to keep a log and report back to you, in detail, all my actions?" Her voice was soft, controlled.

"Where are you?" he demanded, turning as if his sightless eyes would find her.

"Beside the bed." She looked at him and was truly sorry he couldn't see, but that was as far as it went. He had hurt her deeply, dammit. Let him squirm. "What do you think I was doing, Jake? Out soliciting?" Her words sounded childish and the look on his face confirmed it.

"I still want to know why you left so abruptly."

"You and Buck had things to talk about," she said patiently. "Things that didn't concern me." For a fraction of a second she closed her eyes and hated him for making her lie.

"Everything about me concerns you. Everything about you concerns me."

"Not everything." Let him figure that out, damn him.

"I know what's the matter with you. You're ticked off about Liz." His voice rasped queerly.

Surprise held her silent for a moment. Dread lay heavy within her until pride cast it aside.

"I could care less about Liz, Jake. She's your affair, not mine." She said this in a matter-of-fact way that infuriated him.

"Yes, she is my affair." He smiled viciously to hide his anger. "She's been loyal and faithful to me for quite a few years. I can depend on Liz."

"How nice for you," she murmured softly.

He compressed his lips, too angry to answer. The silence hung heavy between them. Lindy placed the sack from the book store on the bed. Jake heard the rustle of the paper.

"So you're leaving," he muttered coolly, turning away from her so she couldn't see his face.

"Not if you want me to stay," she answered equally cool.

"I'm not the type to beg," he snapped.

"I don't expect you to. I came prepared to read to you and it's up to you if I go or stay."

"Stay then, damn you, and read!"

He kept his sightless eyes turned toward the window. He was tired and tense and the bitter lines around his mouth reflected his inner turmoil. This exchange had done nothing to speed his recovery and Lindy promised herself she would try to avoid quarreling with him in

171

the future, for more than anything else in the world she wanted him well again . . . so she could pick up the threads of her own life.

She read to him for over an hour. She read the political news, the report on the progress of the pipeline, the problems the Alaskan conservationists were having with the migrating animals. She read the entire contents of two editorial pages. Jake didn't make a sound, just sat back with his eyes closed. Lindy doubted if he was listening, but she continued to read; her soft Southern voice breaking the silence of the quiet room. When she started the story about the great gray whale in the hunting magazine he interrupted.

"You can stop. You must be thirsty."

"I would like something to drink. Can I get something for you?"

"Yes, please. There's money in the drawer by the bed."

Ignoring what he said about money she picked up her purse and went out.

"I brought you a Coke," she said when she returned and guided a cup into his hand. "They give more ice than Coke in that dispenser."

"Thank you."

She noticed how carefully he lifted the cup to his mouth and felt a flicker of sympathy for him.

"Would you like a radio?"

"No, thank you," he said almost formally. "I'll be getting up every day now. The orderly will be here soon to walk me down the hall. I walked about the room by myself, but I need eyes to guide me when I leave it."

"I can do that."

"No. I won't impose. Not even on my . . . wife."

"If you feel this way, why did you insist on marrying me again? It isn't imposing to ask your wife for help."

"A real wife, yes. But not an accusing, untrusting, suspicious, immature little . . ." He bit the words off and threw the cup containing the soft drink across the room. It hit the wall and splattered the windowpane.

Lindy was stunned momentarily by this display of temper.

"Then you admit our marriage was a mistake?"

"A mistake? Perhaps, but we're married and we're going to stay married. You try leaving me and I'll make you sorry you ever lived!" His lips curled and the puckered scar on his forehead stood out as his face whitened with anger.

She brought a towel from the bathroom. "I'll clean up this mess."

"Leave it."

She continued to clean and when she finished she tried to keep the nervous tremor from her voice when she said, "I'll go, now."

"Go, then! I sure as hell can't stop you."

"I don't want to leave you like this." She

didn't know what made her say that. It just came out.

"Why not? You've left me before. You can't help being the way you are any more than I can help being the way I am. I was wrong. I thought my . . . But forget it. Tuck your tail and run."

"I'll be back in the morning."

"Come here." His voice commanded and she moved toward his outstretched hand. "You're such a paragon of virtue. Come kiss your sightless husband good-bye."

He grabbed her hand roughly and pulled. Trying to avoid his leg on the footstool, she lost her balance and allowed him to pull her down on his lap. He crushed her to him so hard the air exploded from her lungs. His mouth found hers and mastered it cruelly, his teeth cutting into her soft lips. He kissed her long, hard, and when he finally lifted his mouth she could taste the salty blood from the cuts. His hands handled her ruthlessly, bruising, gripping, as though he wanted to hurt her. But she heard the heavy thud of his heart above her own and her body slackened as she listened to it.

Gradually his hands gentled and moved over her, roaming, searching; but she forced herself to lie still, straining to reveal none of the wild and tremulous sensations that quivered into being beneath the adventuring hand that slid into her shirt and over her breast until her nipple was hard in his fingers. She lay passive in his embrace as he kissed her face, going again to her lips which he kissed gently this time. She offered no response and no resistance and presently he loosened his arms and pushed her from his lap.

"Go," he said tiredly.

She left the room without a backward look at the man who sat in the chair by the window.

Lindy walked slowly back to the hotel and tried to convince herself she had made a mistake marrying Jake. She weighed the pros and cons. She heard again Doctor Casey's words that Jake would recover much faster if he was relaxed and free from tension. Her own previous thoughts about grabbing bits and pieces of happiness came to her mind. The lonely nights she had spent with only the sleeping tablets for relief hung in the back of her mind like a black cloud and the time she spent in Jake's arms was the silver lining. She had known what to expect . . . but it had come so soon . . . too soon. Her mother's life flashed before her eyes. She would be walking the same path her mother walked, but unlike her mother, she would never be walked upon. Did she love Jake or hate him?

She drew a warm bath and tried to soak away the nagging feeling of uneasiness inside her. She was nervous and jumpy and on leaving the tub put on her pajamas, crawled into bed and buried her face in the pillow. She didn't want to remember her childhood. She must think of now, the present. A deep, shuddering sigh convulsed her body as the questions throbbed in her brain. Did she love him so much she wouldn't be able to leave him, even knowing what he was? Was she crazy? This morning she hated him.

She pulled the coverlet up over her ears and drifted into a sort of trance. Arousing once she looked at her watch; it was past midnight. Sleep had eluded her during these long miserable hours. Finally a deadly lassitude crept over her and she slept.

She awakened suddenly. The telephone was ringing. Frightened, her trembling hands searched for the light switch. The light sprang on, harsh against her sleep-drugged eyes. With fumbling fingers and pounding heart, she reached for the phone. "Hello."

Silence on the other end while her heart throbbed painfully, then a familiar voice whispered her name. "Lindy."

Her heart rose up in her throat. "Jake? Are you all right?"

Silence, and then, "I'm all right. I just wanted to talk to you. Just wanted to talk to you," he repeated. "But I had to threaten to pull this phone from the wall before they would ring you."

"Oh, Jake. You didn't?" She was so relieved she dropped back on the bed. "What must they think of you?"

"I wanted to hear your voice, sweetheart." The humble tone of his voice and the endearment tore at her heart.

"It's three in the morning. Haven't you slept?"

"Yes . . . no . . . I don't know. It's all the same."

"The same?"

"The darkness. Sweetheart, sometimes I don't think I can bear this darkness." His voice had a catch in it.

She had to swallow the sobs in her throat before she could speak. "It won't be for long, Jake. Doctor Casey is sure . . ."

"He can't be sure!" He said it with rocklike certainty.

"Nothing in life is sure. You said yourself that nothing lasts forever. Remember? There's every reason to believe your sight will return."

There was silence on the other end of the line. Presently he said, "Are you leaving?" There was a darting note of pain in his voice, but she didn't notice, her mind too bewildered by his call.

"Of course not. Whatever gave you that idea?" It suddenly occurred to her that she was about to do that very thing. Run. Get back into her safe cocoon before it was too late.

"You've never asked me what I've been doing the last two years." The words seemed to embarrass him. She wanted to say it was none of her business, but she wanted to know. So she asked the question.

"What have you been doing, Jake?"

"I've been running my butt off!" His voice was bitter. Lindy waited. "I threw caution to the wind and gambled every last dime I had on a played-out oil field. Worked till I dropped in my tracks, chased every woman who turned me on and some that didn't. Denied myself nothing. I found out that there aren't very many women out there that are worth a damn. They'll sleep with you, get a free meal, a few clothes, a couple nights in a swanky hotel, all the time looking for a bigger fish with more clout, more money, more prestige. Do you know what I got out of all that? A sick, empty feeling in my guts! That life out there isn't worth a hoot in hell. I finally realized there was nothing to run after. It's a phony world, sweetheart. A lot crazier and lonelier than anyone can imagine. And one time around is all you get."

He hesitated, then said tiredly, "Then once in a lifetime, during one small speck of time, you get a chance to have everything you ever dreamed of having. The prize goes flashing by and you grab for it. You grab for the whole chunk. If you miss it, you've lost your chance. I don't want that to happen to me. I don't want to lose you, sweetheart. I don't want to wander for a lifetime. That's why I came back. I grabbed and I got you, but I'm selfish. I want it all."

For a moment Lindy couldn't speak, and then, uncomprehending, tears poured down her face. Her voice was a pathetic croak when she spoke at last. "What are you trying to say, Jake?"

"I'm saying, dammit, I don't want you to leave me. I want it to be the way it was. What do you want from me? Do you want me to beg? Plead? Crawl? Ask your forgiveness?"

"No. I don't want any of those things." She was tense, tired, and she was doing what she said she would do. She was trying to keep him quiet, relaxed, free from worry. "I've no intention of leaving until we can go together." Would he believe that? She stammered for words to say. "I was a grouch today. I've developed all kinds of moods these last two years." She laughed a small nervous laugh. "I know I'm not going through the change. Maybe I'm pregnant." She laughed again, hoping it didn't sound too forced, artificial.

"You'd hate that, wouldn't you?" He said it quietly. Then tensely, "You'd beat a path to the nearest clinic and get my baby scraped out of you, wouldn't you, Lindy?"

"Jake!"

He was quiet for a long while. She struggled for something to say. When he spoke his voice was almost a whisper.

"Do you love me at all?"

"There're many kinds of love." Her words were scarcely audible.

"I know that!" He was angry again. "Do you love me in spite of the fact you've got to keep your eye on me every second or I'll go chasing off after another woman? Do you love me like a brother? A friend? Or do you love me because I hold you in the night and chase away the nightmares so you can sleep? It's certainly not like a husband, a lover, a life's companion!"

"If I didn't love you nothing would have made me marry you again. I was free. Remember? Our divorce was final. You had no strings on me at all. Can't you be satisfied with that?"

"Guess I'll have to be. Good night."

"Don't hang up. We've got a whole lifetime to work things out. Let's take one day at a time, shall we? The love, attraction, or whatever it is we have for each other isn't perfect, but it's all we have. It's something to build on. Won't you try?"

"I wish I was out of this damn place. I wish I was there with you. Do you know that I can see you? I can see your mouth. Can taste it. My hands know the shape of your breast, the feel of your hips. Why is the feel of you different from the feel of anyone else?" He didn't expect an answer to his questions. "I know, now, what you mean about the nights being so long."

"Ask the nurse for a sleeping tablet."

"You're not taking them again?" he asked quickly.

"No. But you need to rest." There was a long

pause and her heartbeats quickened uncomfortably.

"I think I want to stay awake." He said it slowly.

"I'll be over the first thing in the morning."

"I wish it was now."

"Good night. I'll be over early."

"Early?"

"Yes. Early."

She waited until she heard the receiver go dead on the other end before she hung up the phone. She turned out the light and buried her head in the pillow. There were many sides to Jake's character, but the one he presented tonight was the most baffling one of all. He had only to say he loved her, that he wanted only her. He had only to say he was not having an affair with Liz and that elusive carrot of happiness would have been dangling before her eyes again.

Chapter Eleven

Jake was released from the hospital the day before they were to leave for Houston. No husband had ever been more tender and attentive than he had been during the past week. It was a reprieve. Jake was good at reprieves.

Coming into the hospital room to escort him to the hotel, Lindy paused to look at her husband standing beside the window, his proud head erect, his shoulders set in an arrogant line, his neatly trimmed hair already rebelling against the stiff brush that had tried to discipline it.

"Jake?"

No answer, but a smile of gladness spread across his face and he held out his arms to her. She went into them and was locked in a gentle, tender embrace. All was peace, she was home. Releasing a deep and trembling sigh she raised her lips to receive his kiss.

"I'm only half alive until you get here," he murmured in her ear. Her arms crept around him beneath his coat, and her hands caressed his back. His lips hovered fractionally above hers. "When we get to the hotel I'm going to attack you!"

Just as their lips met, Buck's familiar drawl broke in. "Hey, now! A serpent has just creeped into the garden of Eden."

Jake kissed her one more time and reluctantly let her go. "Hello, serpent," he said dryly.

Lindy moved out of his arms, but not away from him. "Hello, Buck," she said.

"Howdy." He came into the room. "Sorry to be a buttin' in on you-all, but I need to tell the man a few things before I go."

Lindy led Jake to a chair and waited until he was seated. She stood beside him, her hand on his shoulder. "Are you leaving us?"

"I haven't had a chance to tell her." Jake's hand came up to find hers and his fingers interlaced with her fingers. "Buck's leaving me in your care, Mama. Think you can get me on the plane and keep me from spilling soup on my tie?"

"Your tie? More than likely I'll be keeping the soup off your Astro T-shirt!" He was holding her hand so tight it hurt.

"I'm a Dallas Cowboy fan, you dumb-dumb!"

"Well, you're breaking this dummy's hand, cowboy."

"Sorry." He loosened his hold and they both laughed.

"Can I have my say?" Buck was impatient. "That little old cab driver has got to get me to the airport in twenty minutes."

"Say it, Buck. Did you talk to Mary Ellen?"

"Sure did. I'm going to Mexico City and help her get things lined up so she can come back home."

"Did you tell her that I'll rent a beach house for her and the boys? I want my wife and my sister to get to know each other. Running a tourist business in a foreign country is no job for a widow with a couple of kids. She's been alone since she married that good-for-nothing. Do what you can, Buck, and send the bills to Liz."

Buck handed Lindy an envelope. "Here's your tickets, and some cash to see you through. Your flight leaves in the morning. The time is there on the envelope. Take plenty of time to get to the airport, honey. The roads get bad sometimes. The hotel and hospital bills have been paid. I'm taking your big cases with me and I'll have Carlos take them on down to the beach house. All you've got to mess with is the things in your hotel room and the man here."

"We'll be fine, Buck. Thanks for everything."

"Have Carlos meet us." Jake let go of Lindy's hand to shake Buck's when he felt his touch.

" 'Bye, Buck." Lindy watched him leave the room, then looked down at Jake. A broad smile began to take over his face.

"Call the taxi, woman. We got things to do. I plan to spend the whole day in bed."

They almost did.

The long flight back to Houston was smooth and comfortable. Their first-class accommodations were roomy and Jake could stretch his injured leg. He had reluctantly submitted to the chair lift that hoisted him into the plane and the flight steward guided him to his seat. When Lindy joined them the man was just moving away and the forced smile left Jake's face, and as she watched, his features, so dark and strong, sobered. There was something strangely vulnerable about him. It was as though he had shed the hard facade he had cloaked himself with just after the accident. A rush of emotion engulfed her; how she both loved and hated this man!

"You're awfully quiet," Jake said after she had been sitting beside him for a while. "Are you tired?"

"A little. I didn't get much sleep last night."

He sought her hand and held it to his cheek, before bringing it to his mouth and nipping her fingers lightly with his teeth.

"Did you mind?"

"Not a darn bit!" she whispered wickedly.

"Is anyone looking?"

"And if there is?" she teased.

"Then they're in for a treat. I'm going to kiss you anyway."

She reached up and removed the dark glasses from his face. His arms encircled her and he kissed her with infinite tenderness, yet with a hint of fervor that excited her. His hand caressed her intimately and his kiss changed, deepening to a searching delight. Her lips parted, accepting the sweetness, curving with gentle passion.

He lifted his head to speak. "I'm the world's biggest fool."

"Fool?" Fear welled blackly in her mind. Dear God! What now?

"A fool to be so happy," he said slowly in her ear. "I've got a beautiful wife in my arms that I can't see, in a place where I can't make proper love to her, and a broken leg to restrain me. And I'm still happy!"

It was in the middle of the morning when the big plane landed at the Houston airport. Lindy and Jake waited until the other passengers had left the plane before attempting to exit. The stewardess reminded them of the warm weather outside and they turned their coats over to the porter who came aboard to carry off their hand luggage. Jake laughingly refused the offer of a wheelchair to help speed them through the airport.

"My wife leads me around by the nose," he teasingly told the pilot and copilot who had come back to shake hands with him and wish him a speedy recovery.

The pilot stared at Lindy with open invitation in his eyes, admiring her slender figure. Her shirt was tucked smoothly into the waist of her flared skirt, her hair carefully brushed and turned into just the right curve, her eyes bright blue against the whiteness of her skin, untouched for many months by the sun's hot rays.

"Not a bad way to go," he murmured to Jake while still looking at Lindy.

At last they were stepping down upon Texas soil, to familiar scents and sounds, to a sense of excitement that banished the tiredness of travel. The sun was warm on their faces and Lindy's eyes squinted against the unaccustomed brightness. She searched the waiting crowd for someone who would be meeting them until the immediate problem of getting through the airport security demanded her attention.

"I don't see anyone that could be Carlos," she said to Jake when they had passed the inspection point and entered the lobby.

"Don't worry. He'll be here. Take me to some out-of-the-way spot and I'll wait for you to find the porter and our luggage. He'll be here by then."

She led him to a less crowded area and found a place where he could sit without the danger of someone falling over his outstretched leg. Reluctant to leave him, she went toward the baggage room in search of the porter. He found her before she found him and loaded with their hand luggage and heavy coats he followed her back down the lobby. The seat where she had left Jake was empty when she reached it. Her heart missed a beat then palpitated rapidly as her frantic eyes searched for him.

She saw him almost immediately standing not far away, but her relief was short-lived and in its place she felt dark, smoldering anger. Standing close to him, gazing adoringly into his sightless eyes, was Liz, her two hands clutching his arm possessively.

The petite figure in the flimsy sundress that left her brown shoulders bare was the recipient of every male eye that passed her. The silvery blond hair that had been long two years ago was now cut in a modish style and swung gently about her neck. She teetered provocatively on the slender heels of her sandals as she leaned toward Jake talking earnestly.

Lindy stopped dead in her tracks. The porter coming around from behind to look questioningly at her stared at her stricken face, the smile leaving his lips. For one moment she wished fervently a crack would appear and swallow her up. Instinctively she turned away and her eyes met those of the porter. She wanted to leave, to get away, but . . . she couldn't! She looked back at Jake and knew she didn't have the strength to go to him voluntarily. She stood there too numb to speak or move.

Through the ringing of bells in her ears and

the normal sounds of the airport lobby, she heard a trilling voice calling her name. "Lindy. Lindy, we're over here."

She moved toward the voice.

"Lindy?" Jake turned his head from one side to the other. Making an effort to control her shattered nerves she stood beside him. "I'm here and the porter is with me." She was dazed at the way the calm words fell from her mouth without difficulty.

"It's nice to see you again, Lindy."

Lindy's eyes swung toward the voice. The soft, sweet Southern voice came from a girl whose face was cold and still, whose eyes shot undisguised hatred at her. Her mouth was set in a defiant line and her fingers still clutched at Jake's arm.

"Where's Buck?" Lindy asked through stiff lips.

"Buck left for Mexico this morning, Jake." Liz's voice played false to the look of her face. "He asked me to meet you when something came up to prevent Carlos from coming."

"What came up?"

"Oh, something about Maria. You know how Mexican men are about their pregnant wives."

"Did Mary Ellen call?"

"She called and they talked for a long while. I think he decided to go suddenly." Liz shook Jake's arm gently. "We just may have a romance on our hands."

"That would be great!" His hand came up to

squeeze the hand on his arm. Liz laughed lightly as if she and Jake were sharing a secret and Lindy burned with resentment.

"I'd like nothing better for Mary Ellen," Jake said. "Buck would be just right for her and the boys."

A cold knot settled in Lindy's stomach. This intimate conversation was designed to exclude her and the triumphant look Liz threw at her told her she knew of her annoyance.

Feeling hot and gauche beside the cool-looking Liz, Lindy's temper flared. "The porter has been waiting long enough, Jake, unless you want to make it worth his while to stand and listen to you two."

Jake turned toward her, a frown creasing his forehead.

"I'm sorry, Lindy," Liz said, her voice dripping sweetness. "You're hot in that heavy skirt and it's mean of me to make you wait. It's just that Jake and I have so much to talk about, I completely forgot how uncomfortable you are." She looked Lindy up and down. "Let's be off, Jake. I pulled all sorts of strings to get us a parking spot nearby so you wouldn't have so far to walk."

Jake turned, obediently, and let Liz lead him toward the door. Lindy and the porter followed.

Keeping up a constant chatter to Jake and solicitous of his safety to a sickening degree, Liz led the procession out of the building and toward a white Lincoln Continental parked close to the curb.

"I brought the Lincoln, Jake. The right seat will slide back far enough to make room for your leg."

"Good thinking. But I knew you'd have things under control."

With a look of victory on her face, Liz helped Jake into the car. Why am I allowing this? Lindy thought crazily. But then again why should I assert myself? As long as he has her what does he need with me? Why don't I turn tail and run? There's no one to stop me.

The porter asked for the keys and unlocked the trunk to stow away the luggage and coats. There were two cases already in the compartment and glancing at them Lindy felt once again a choking sensation in her throat. Humbly she paid the porter and moved around to get into the back seat of the car. Liz started the motor and they moved away from the curb and into the stream of traffic.

"All set, sweetheart?" Jake broke into Liz's prattle and extended his hand back for Lindy to take.

"All set." She touched his hand briefly, then recoiled from it as if it burned her.

"You're hot and tired." He said it as if offering an excuse for her silence.

She didn't answer and looked out of the window at the line of moving cars and wished she was anywhere, except where she was.

"Check the air vent, sweetheart. You must open the vent to get cool air back there." Jake persisted in talking to her.

The sun was beaming into the window and Lindy could feel the trickles of moisture running down her neck and between her breasts. The wool skirt, which had been so necessary in Fairbanks, was now a weight against her thighs. She was hot and uncomfortable, she was weak, she was angry, she was scared.

They moved out of the city traffic and onto the interstate highway toward Galveston. Lindy grudgingly admitted Liz handled the big car well. But why shouldn't she, she thought angrily. She probably has the use of it anytime she wants.

Liz kept a continual conversation going with Jake about subjects Lindy couldn't have talked about if she wanted to, which she didn't. Liz held a responsible position in Jake's company and they talked at length about company business.

"Now, Jake," Liz was saying in a cool, confident business voice, "Buck need not stay in the office. I'll be able to manage. You'll need him on the road or over at the branch office. I'll be your eyes until you are able to see again. I'll read the contracts to you and we can decide the best way to handle them. As a matter of fact, I brought some things with me that need your immediate attention. And oh, I forgot to tell you that Carlos and I fixed up the small bedroom as an office for you to use until you can come back to the city." Without waiting for Jake to comment, she continued, "I've had a wonderful time arranging the house. I've spent every weekend down there and I think you'll like what I've done. Only one package came that I really didn't like and that was the sheets for the big bed. Can you imagine white sheets with small blue flowers? I took them back and told that silly girl what I thought of them and exchanged them for solid blue ones."

"I ordered white sheets with small blue flowers for that bed," Jake said quietly. "I liked them."

"Oh, I'm sorry. Truly I am." Liz's voice was choked as if she was going to cry.

"It's all right. Don't worry about it. We appreciate you giving up your weekends to straighten up the house."

"I was glad to do it. I've loved that house from the day we first came down to look at it." Liz glanced into the driver's mirror to see if Lindy had caught the implication of her words.

Lindy sat stiffly, numbly, expressionlessly. There is a plateau of suffering which, once reached, results in a blessed state of numbness. The comments about the furnishing of the house had forced Lindy to accept the fact the relationship between Liz and her husband was as strong as she suspected and that she meant so little to him that he made no attempt to hide it.

Questions swirled in her mind. What was his reason for coming to Alaska to get her? The divorce was final. Why couldn't he have let it go at that? Why did he say he had bought the house for her, when Liz had been consulted about the purchase and had been in charge of the furnishings?

"Lindy . . ." Jake's voice jarred into her consciousness. He had turned in the seat and the hand that reached her skin was tugging at it to get her attention. "Are you asleep, we'll be there soon. Liz says we're about a mile away. I'm anxious for you to see the house."

The house! The damn house! Any interest she had in the house had been drained away from her. Liz's subtle insinuations had taken care of that. He could do as he damn well wanted with his house.

"You must be hot." Jake's voice droned on, falling on Lindy's ears like a recording. "As soon as we get home you can take a shower and get into something cool. Buck sent your trunk down before he left for Mexico."

Lindy looked down at the hand on her skirt, the hand that had handled so efficiently the monstrous truck and the hand that had gripped hers when he had called for her in his delirium, the hand that wore the wedding ring she bought for him just minutes before she bought her wedding dress.

"I'll do that," she said, because she had to say something.

"Where are we now, Liz?"

"The house is just ahead on the left. I'm turning into the drive now. I'll park here on the side and Carlos can get our cases out before he takes the car to the garage. It's all right, isn't it, if I stay a day or two? Buck suggested . . . we thought . . ." Her voice trailed off waveringly.

Jake was silent, then said, "Buck suggested you stay?"

"He'll pick me up as soon as he gets back. We have so much work to do and you will have decisions to make regarding the contracts I'll read to you. I promise I'll stay out of the way."

Lindy sat there trembling for a minute that seemed an hour. She wanted to scream out that she could stay forever as far as she was concerned. She wouldn't last with Jake any longer than any other woman. Nothing lasts forever. Not you, Liz. Not me. Not even a lie. Damn you, Jake. You used me. You took my heart, my faith, my vulnerability, and you used me. But I'm in my home territory now, damn you, and you'll not grind me down.

Chapter Twelve

Jake opened the door and got out of the car. He felt for the handle of the back door so he might assist Lindy. He couldn't seem to locate the lever so she pushed the door open and got out. Standing by the car she turned her face toward the gulf and the gentle breeze cooled her face and lifted her hair. The sound of the surf and the ever-present seagulls were dear and familiar as were the wide expanse of water and the fishing boats headed for port.

"*Señor, señor!*" A short Mexican man came out of the house. His words ran together in his excitement.

"Carlos!" There was a warm ring to Jake's voice and a smile on his face as he held out his hand.

"*Señor,* I glad you come home." Carlos gripped Jake's hand.

Jake reached a groping hand out for Lindy and although she made no effort to meet it he caught her arm and drew her forward.

"My wife, Carlos. Her name is Lindy."

The plump, pleasant face of the man looked up at Lindy for he was rather short. He smiled, showing white teeth beneath a bushy black mustache.

"Pleaz to meet cha, *señora*."

"Thank you."

"Where's Maria, Carlos?"

"Oh, she come, *señor*. She kinda fat, can't run fast like Carlos."

Jake laughed. "She hasn't had the baby yet?"

"Not yet, *señor*," Carlos said disgustedly. "I think maybe she have it yesterday, but it was false alarm."

His wife appeared suddenly from around the car. They were perfectly matched. She was a little shorter than he was and very pregnant.

"Oh, *señor!*" Tears were actually streaming down over her plump cheeks. "You poor eyes!"

"Maria." Jake reached for her. "Do I dare hug you?" He held her shoulders and bent to place a kiss on her wet cheek.

Liz, standing quietly on the other side of the car, had instant disapproval on her face at this display of affection.

"This is Lindy, my wife," Jake said, his hand searching for her.

Maria turned questioning eyes to Jake before turning big solemn ones to Lindy.

"*Señora* Williamson," she said shyly.

"Call me Lindy for I'm not going to call you *Señora* Santos."

A smile appeared on the smooth brown face. Brown eyes sparkled and went quickly to her husband and then back to Lindy and around the car apprehensively. Following her gaze

Lindy saw that Liz had disappeared.

"Let's get inside out of the sun." Jake reached again to Lindy, but she avoided his hand and turned away.

"I'll go ahead with Maria. Carlos will guide you." She deftly sidestepped around Jake and headed for the house.

Maria led her through a screened veranda porch that ran the full width of the front of the house facing the gulf. The house was set high off the ground to catch the cool breeze and several steps were climbed to reach the veranda. Large double doors led into the main room which was extremely large. All the furniture in the room was white wicker with seats and backs covered with a yellow-and-blue-flowered material. The blue on the furniture matched perfectly the all-over blue carpet on the floor. The room was bright and casual-looking and she wanted to hate it, but she couldn't. It was the picture she had cut from *Better Homes and Gardens* come to life.

The kitchen was perfect. All stark white except for the copper utensils hanging above an island countertop stove. A small glassed-in eating area connected with the kitchen.

Maria glanced anxiously at the silent girl who looked as though she had neither like nor dislike for her new home. "You like?"

"It's very nice," Lindy assured her.

Maria looked relieved and led her down the hall, opening doors as she went along. "This big room." Her eyes twinkled up at Lindy. It was a large square room done in gold and brown and was dominated by a king-size bed. "Nice?"

"Nice." Lindy's voice was flat, but it seemed to satisfy Maria who opened the door next to the master bedroom. Liz stood beside the bed unpacking her cases. She looked up frowning.

" 'Scuse, *señorita*." Maria quickly closed the door and proceeded down the hall. "Next room is little one and now office."

The fourth and last bedroom, the one at the back of the house, was large and also square. The windows were covered with frilly yellow curtains. The furnishings were French provincial, the bedspread layers of ruffles. The only thing missing was a doll with a voluptuous skirt in the middle of the bed. A ten-year-old girl would have loved the room.

"The *señorita* say put your things here," Maria said with a note of apology in her voice. "Say *señor* must have rest in big bed."

Lindy felt a surge of anger, then relief that she need not share a room with Jake. "It's all right. Is there a bath?"

"*Sí*. Baths with all rooms, but little one."

"I think I'll shed these clothes and have a cool bath."

Smiling shyly, Maria went to the door. Lindy followed her and turned the small knob that locked it. Her head throbbed, her body ached. Voices, faces, moments crowded into her head, panic tore at her heart in a way she couldn't bear. She sat in solitary silence on the edge of the bed for half an hour, thinking, trying not to let her mind drift back to the tender moments she had shared with Jake.

Leaving her clothes in a heap on the floor she stepped into the shower. Standing under the cooling stream she allowed the full pressure of the water to beat at her body. She was utterly weary. Weary to the bone. She clung to the heavy handles of the water controls, half awake, half dreaming for uncountable minutes until the water turned icy cold. Slowly she turned it off and reached for the fluffy towel and began to rub herself vigorously to get rid of the chill of the icy water. Wrapping the towel around her she went back into the bedroom.

Taking fresh underwear from the drawer in the bureau, she glanced into the mirror. Jake was standing quietly, his back against the closed door. He had removed the dark glasses and his sightless eyes were looking straight at her. It was unbelievable he couldn't see, uncanny that he could pinpoint her exact location.

"Well!" she blurted. Did he want a showdown now?

"What are you doing in here?" The tone of his voice was a weapon in itself. It savaged her, sending a shiver of dread down her spine, leaving her shaking.

"Taking a shower." From deep within her nature she scooped up enough courage to say it with exaggerated patience.

"I may be blind, but I'm not deaf. I knew you were taking a shower. I want to know why you are in this room." She saw the tremor pass over his hard face.

She was like ice now. "I'm in this room because your *friend* had my things brought to this room. 'She thought you too sick' . . . and 'need rest in big bed,' to use Maria's words. For once I agree with her. Liz won't take up near the space I would." She had thrown pride to the wind because now this conflict was too bitter for her to bear.

"You'll allow my *friend* to come into your home and take over?"

My home? I had nothing to do with this house, for God's sake! She wanted to scream — instead she merely shrugged her shoulders, forgetting for the moment he could not see.

"Answer me, damn you!" he jerked out. His face was white and his hands clenched. Despite her anger she saw him, like a caged tiger, immobilized, without a hand to guide him, and she felt a small prickle of pity.

"Lindy!" Her name was a hiss as it came from his lips.

She was incapable of replying anything except a stream of accusations so she stood silently as if glued to the floor. In the silence her anger left her and she wanted to cry. It was like two years ago all over again only a million times worse.

"Very well. Stay here! But don't lock this door. I'll not ask Carlos again for a key to my wife's room. I'll kick it down!"

After a moment, when she didn't answer, he opened the door and limped out, closing it softly behind him.

She seemed to stand there for an eternity after he left, watching a sliver of sunlight on the floor. She didn't move, she didn't think, didn't feel. Her mind dozed like the sunlight. She was numb. She lay down across the bed and relaxed her body, willed her mind to stay in limbo and went to sleep.

She awakened refreshed and resigned to the direction her life had taken during the last twelve hours. She slipped into a cool sundress and pushed her bare feet into brief sandals. Standing before the mirror she looked at herself critically. True, her brown hair needed a trim, but it was shiny and smooth and lay snug against her cheeks. Her skin was clear and pale from months spent without sunshine and she resolved to spend time on the beach to add a golden tone to her skin as well as absent herself from the house. She added a touch of color to her lips and as was her habit a dab of perfume to her throat and left the sanctuary of the bedroom.

Liz's voice was coming from the small room that had been converted into an office. As she passed the open door she could see her sitting in a chair, her legs crossed provocatively, reading from a legal document. All she could see of Jake was the back of his head and one brown hand holding a cigarette. It struck her odd for Jake to be smoking, for as far as she could recall he had never smoked.

She went on down the hall, her footsteps silent on the thick carpet, and into the large main room of the house. Pausing inside the door she looked around. When she had first looked at the room her mind had been so confused she hadn't grasped the full meaning that came to her now. The room was the exact replica of a room they had looked at in the window of a furniture store years ago. They had talked about the room and the furniture for days. It was unbelievable to her that he would remember and use this devious method to exact his punishment.

The room was lovely. Lindy reluctantly admitted it was the loveliest room she had ever seen. A white wicker stand, topped with a large green Boston fern caught her eye. It was placed too near the large windows. The green fern would soon die in the direct rays of the merciless sun. She almost gasped with pleasure when she saw the miniature orange tree, with small yellow oranges hanging from its small limbs. It was growing in a large wooden tub beside the fireplace. She had always had a fondness for growing things. Her apartment in the city had been filled with flourishing house plants. With all these beautiful plants to care for she could come to love this house and hate to leave it.

She went through the swinging doors and into the kitchen. Maria was sitting on a high stool by the sink and Carlos was cleaning vegetables. Maria was scolding. He was laughing and teasing her. The Mexican girl looked up and the smile left her face when she saw Lindy. She climbed off the stool and Carlos turned to find the reason for her silence.

"I help Maria. Her back hurt from big *niño*." A sparkle of adoration lit his dark eyes when he looked at his wife.

The arrangement of the work space was ideal. Lindy cautioned herself not to get to liking it too much. She had learned during the last two years not to let herself get attached to anything. Leaving was too painful.

The couple's eyes caught and held. They were so obviously in love. How lucky they were. A merciless pain stabbed Lindy's heart.

"Will you help me move the fern stand back from the window, Carlos? The fern will die if left there in the sun."

Carlos and his wife exchanged glances. "I will help, *señora,* but . . . I move it one time and the *señorita,* she make me move it back." He shook his head and an anxious look came over his face. "She be mad."

Lindy's head came up. A wave of anger hit

her. "Well, now, that will be just too bad, won't it?"

"Sure!" Carlos beamed and headed for the door.

It was almost evening. Lindy stood by the big window watching a small shrimp boat, riding low in the water, heading for home port. Jake and Liz came into the room. She tensed and forced herself to turn around. She was dying inside, but they would never know.

"Careful, honey. Carlos has moved the fern again." Liz guided Jake around it. "I'll mix you a drink."

Jake stopped and stood perfectly still. "Lindy?" He waited. "Lindy, I know you're in here. I smell your perfume."

"I moved the fern," she said firmly. She was controlled, her feelings in limbo. She had expected to be nervous, angry.

"Do you like the view?" Jake asked quietly.

"Very much."

"Would you like a drink?"

"No, thank you." How could they be so damned civilized? She wanted to laugh till she saw the smirk on Liz's face.

"Shall we have our drink, Jake?"

"By all means have your drink and Carlos will serve your dinner."

"And you, Lindy?" Jake was holding a tight rein on himself. She knew he wanted to explode.

"I've had dinner with Carlos and Maria. I'll

take a walk down the beach while you and your . . . *friend* have dinner." Let him chew on that for a while.

She could see the effort he was making to control his anger. His face turned white, then red, and he ground his teeth together rather than make an angry retort.

"If that's what you want." He shrugged his shoulders. "I'll have that drink now, Liz. You know what I want."

Liz laughed. "I should know by now."

Lindy saw the satisfied look on Liz's face as she moved past them and went out onto the veranda. She hoped and prayed Jake's sight would return soon so she could leave, for those two truly deserved each other.

She walked a mile down the beach. The wind blowing from the gulf sent the waves scampering onto the sandy shore and if her mind had not been busy she would have enjoyed the feel of it against her hot face. Far down the beach a bonfire blazed. Laughter and music drifted on the breeze and when the sound reached her it seemed unreal. It was almost sacrilegious, somehow, that people could be happy, laugh, have fun.

She walked slowly back as if to postpone for as long as possible another meeting with Jake and Liz. What could he possibly say in defense of the position he had put her in? God! Why don't I have the courage to walk out into that water and never come back? She whispered the words into the wind and her sad eyes looked out to where the blue water met the darkening sky.

It was dark when she walked up the steps to the veranda. She could see the glow of a cigarette at the far end and wondered if Jake was alone. She doubted it. Liz wouldn't leave him to sit alone. It was too good an opportunity to miss. She would be sitting there beside him, chatting lightly, showering him with attention, making it obvious to him that she and not his wife was looking out for him. Silently Lindy went through the door and down the hall to her room, grateful once again to escape them.

She sat on the edge of the bed and dialed Debra's number. When the familiar voice answered it was as if the years had never been and they were once again back in high school.

"It's me, Debbie. How are you?"

"Lindy! For God's sake! I just got your letter. Where are you?"

"Galveston. We got in this morning. I didn't have time to call you from Houston."

"What's wrong? You don't sound happy."

"Happy? I've never been so miserable in my whole life, for chrissake! I'm coming in tomorrow. Will you be home?"

"After ten. I've got to take my youngest in for a shot. I'll be home after that. What's wrong, Lindy? Are you sorry you married Jake again? How could things have gone sour so soon?"

"I'll tell you about it tomorrow, Debbie. How're the kids? How's Jean?"

"The kids are fine, Mom's fine. Is Jake still unable to see?"

"His sight hasn't returned, but it will. The doctor in Alaska is almost sure it will return. Have you seen anything of my . . . dad?" She hurried on as if she needed to give an excuse for asking about her father. "I want to get some things out of the house. My trunk, some pictures, things like that."

"Your dad and Marilyn are living at the house, Lindy. They've redone it. It looks real nice. Of course I've only seen the outside. Mom says your dad seems happy. Looks years younger."

"Good for him!" The words came sharply, bitterly. Debra didn't say anything and presently Lindy asked, "Did you find any place suitable for my needlework shop?"

"You're going ahead with that?"

"Of course I am. I've got to do something, Debbie. I'll see you tomorrow and tell you about it. I don't know yet how I'm going to get there, but if necessary I'll take a taxi to the bus station."

"Are things so bad?"

"Worse than you can imagine."

"I'll see you tomorrow, then. 'Bye."

After Lindy hung up the phone she lay back on the bed and wished the night away. Debbie had been the one permanent thing in her life.

From grade school through high school and into the working years before either of them married, Debbie had always been there; solid, dependable, never inclined to go off the deep end about anything. She had married first, falling in love with Brian who was just exactly as tall as she was. They had a house in the suburbs, a stationwagon, two boys. Debbie belonged to the PTA, the Women's Club and a sorority. She was as sublimely content with her life as Lindy was dissatisfied with hers.

She was startled when the door opened. Jake came in, closed it behind him and leaned back languidly, but his face was hard. His eyes were concealed behind his glasses, but the set of his mouth told her that if she could see them they would be murderous.

"Do you want me to kill you?" he asked almost wearily.

"There are times when I would almost welcome it." It was the first truly honest thing she had said all day and he ignored it.

"Who were you calling? Kenfield? Crying on his shoulder because you're stuck with a blind husband? I thought the house, the money, would make up for being married to me."

Lindy felt humiliation burning her face, but knowing he was in a dangerous mood kept her voice calm.

"I called Debbie. I'm going in to see her tomorrow. I haven't seen her in almost a year. I also want to get some of my things from . . .

home." She hesitated before saying the last word. Home was gone, for heaven's sake! She had no home, no roots, no anything, but Debbie.

His ears, sharpened by his inability to see, heard her move off the bed. "Stay here!" he said tensely.

"I wasn't leaving."

"Is the light on?"

"Yes."

"Good. Then you know my intentions." He began to unbutton his shirt.

"I don't want you here, Jake," she burst out with burning panic in her voice. "I won't sleep with you again . . . ever!"

"You think not?" His lips twisted into a sneer. "My dear wife, you say the most amusing things."

"I mean it. I don't want you in here." What was he trying to do to her? Anger, fear, made her reckless. "What do you want with me, Jake? You've got a willing woman just down the hall."

"I like a variety," he said insolently.

"I won't stay here!"

"You make an attempt to leave this room and I'll . . . I'll break every bone in your body!" The lamp light seemed to drain the color from his skin.

"Jake!" She gazed at him with the dilated eyes of surprise that he would make such a threat. "Jake!" she said again and for the first time since she had known him she felt a stab of fear; he was so big and dark standing there by the door and the unbuttoned shirt and clenched fist added to his power.

"I'm sorry. I'm sorry, Lindy. I didn't mean that." Very deliberately he pulled a package of cigarettes from his pocket and put one in his mouth. He brought a lighter and with a flick of his thumb the flame appeared. Lindy watched in fascination his attempt to find the end of the cigarette. He missed his mark and the flame came dangerously close to his face.

"Wait." She caught his wrist and took the lighter from him and held it to the end of the cigarette dangling from his lips. He took a deep pull on it and drew down the smoke before releasing it from his taut nostrils. The lamp light gleamed on his thick hair, played over his stoical features.

"I didn't know you smoked."

"There's a lot of things about me you don't know and never cared enough to find out. I learned to enjoy smoking in South America. I've been trying to quit."

There didn't seem to be anything she could say to that. She put the lighter in his hand. Before she could move away his fingers grasped her wrist.

"Where's the bed?"

"Go back to your room, Jake. You're not going to stay here."

"I'm staying here whether you like it or not."

His fingers tortured her wrist. "I'll not suffer the humiliation of having my wife, my loving bride," he said sneeringly, "kick me out of her bed on our first night home because she's peeved that my secretary had things that needed my immediate attention."

"Jake! Do you think I'm . . . stupid?"

"Where's the bed?" he asked quietly and followed when she led him across the room. When he felt the mattress against his legs he dropped her wrist and his hand moved on her breast.

"Don't!" she hissed. His hand continued to move up and down her body, stroking away the thin material of her nightdress. "Please, Jake, don't!" She put out urgent hands to hold him off, but as soon as they touched his chest she withdrew them and tried to find his wrist. He leaned over her, pushing her deeper into the soft bed, and his mouth sought hers and took possession, moving gently yet expertly, coaxing a response. She refused to part her lips and he bit her, the involuntary cry opening her mouth and she was forced to allow him entrance.

Lindy felt sick. Sick with guilt for wanting him. Sick because she knew what he felt for her was lust. Sick because the smell of his skin, his hair, and the sweet wine of his kisses made her mind spin senselessly. Her heart was racing, thundering in her ears, and her body tautened until she felt she would explode with the agony of desire.

"Let yourself go, sweetheart. Jump into the darkness with me." Low, husky whispers came to her ears. "Believe in me . . . trust me . . . love me."

"Love you?" Her voice came out in a shaken whisper because his lips were tormenting hers, moving on to her ear, to the pulse beating so frantically in her throat. "You don't love me. You just . . . want me."

"Wanting is loving," he said softly, his lips nibbling hers, his voice a shivering whisper. "That's how it is with us. Don't throw it away."

"No," she groaned and the thought of never having this pleasure again made her wince. "There's more to it than this."

"There could be." His hard cheek was pressed into the softness of hers. "Give us time and we'll have it." She parted her lips to the flicker of his because that was what she wanted to do. "I want you now and you want me," the seductive voice droned on in her ear. "I know you want me. I can tell by the way you're touching me. I'm drunk with the way you feel beneath me and I don't think I can wait much longer . . ."

The tides of their passion for each other met and swirled together and once again she seemed to drown in a flood of sensuous feelings, only to surface to lie close to him, tears of frustration wetting his chest.

Chapter Thirteen

Lindy." Many times she had dreamed she heard Jake calling to her, calling gently, teasingly, as if they were children playing in a dark wood.

"Lindy." Her name was a soft whisper wooing her from the depths of sleep, cajoling her to wakefulness. She wasn't going to open her eyes. She didn't want to awaken, because in sleep there was no regret, no guilt, no pain. She pressed her naked body closer to the warm length against her and snuggled her cheek against the muscled chest.

"Lindy." The voice was a little louder, more urgent. "Wake up and tell me what time it is."

Reluctantly she opened her eyes and pushed tangled hair back from her sleep-flushed face. She freed an arm from the soft confines of the sheet that covered them and pushed herself up and away from Jake. It was morning. The sun streamed in through the yellow curtains.

"I'm sorry I had to wake you, but much as I would like to, I can't lie here another minute. My leg is killing me." He sat up and swung his leg off the bed. "What time is it?"

"Seven o'clock."

His naked back and buttocks were toward her and she was flooded suddenly with a sense of shame as the memory of the ecstasy she had experienced with him came rushing back. Jake felt around on the floor for his clothes. She turned over, not wanting to see his naked male body.

"I think I'd better go see if I can get another cast put on this leg. Dammit . . . it's a damn nuisance! I can't see, can't walk . . . I'm in a hell of a mess." She felt his weight on the bed as he sat down again. His hand moved up to her body to her head and he knew her face was turned away from him. He fingered her hair and laughed suddenly. "Guess I shouldn't complain. I'm not impotent." She didn't say anything and finally he said, "Is the door straight ahead?"

"Ahead and a little to the right. There's nothing in the way."

"Thank you," he said coolly. She turned her head and watched him grope his way to the door.

Lindy didn't get to Debra's until noon. Jake had insisted she take the small car and go, because his appointment with the doctor wasn't until two o'clock and Carlos would drive him in the Lincoln. Liz would stay with Maria because Carlos was reluctant to leave her alone. The baby was due any day now. Liz was not happy with the arrangement, not that

215

it mattered to Lindy. She was relieved to be away from her, from Jake and the house.

She and Debra hugged each other, stood away and looked each other over and hugged again.

"You're thinner and I'm fatter," Debra wailed.

"You look great."

"Liar. If I looked like a tub you'd say I looked great."

"No, I'd say, 'Hey there, tub, it's good to see you.'"

"We've got hours to talk. I sent one monster to the 'Y' and the other to playschool."

"I'm anxious to see the boys. Have they grown?"

"Like weeds. I've got drinks ready. You'll have to take a diet cola and you don't even need it, dammit."

An hour later Lindy hadn't finished her first glass of cola and Debra had finished her third plus a plate of cookies.

"No one in the whole world makes cookies like you do, Debbie."

"No one eats them like I do either, but you know how I am when I get all steamed up about something. I eat. You've really had it, Lindy. How can a guy be as good to look at as Jake is and be so bad?"

"It isn't that he's so bad, Debbie. We just don't go together. Sometimes I think I'll fly into a million pieces."

"How about using some of that assertiveness training you took? Have you ever thought about going back down there and telling Liz to get her butt out of your house and telling Jake that you don't have to put up with all that monkey business?"

"I've thought about it, but assertiveness in the classroom is one thing, putting it to use is another."

"What do you have to lose? Lay it on the line. Either she goes or you do. It's as simple as that. To tell you the truth I think Jake is crazy about you, has always been. I was surprised when he let you go without putting up more of a fight. I've always liked Jake. So has Brian. We couldn't believe he went to bed with Liz right on your living-room couch. By the way, what did Jake have to say about that?"

"He said he was drunk and she brought him home. I couldn't bring myself to tell him that I knew the rest of what happened that night. It was too humiliating."

"That's the pit of the whole thing!" Debra untangled her short legs and got up off the sofa to pace the floor. "You and Jake don't communicate. Brian and I tell each other everything. You've got to have it out with Jake. Clear the air. Tell him you love him, but you'll not put up with any more fooling around. He must love you a powerful lot to come all the way to Alaska to get you. Don't shake your head at me, Lindy Williamson. I know you're insane about him and have been since the day you met him. But, love, don't let him use your love as a weapon against you. Just say to him, 'This is the way it's going to be, buster, like it or lump it.' You'll have to decide for yourself if you can forgive him. No one can help you."

"Oh, Debbie. You make things sound so simple."

"I'm a good talker when it's someone else's life. Frankly if it was my life and Jake was my husband I'd kill him."

Lindy left with a sack of cookies and the promise that Debbie would bring the boys down the next weekend.

"But I'll call before I come," she called as Lindy backed out of the driveway.

She drove the few blocks to her old home. It was crazy, but when she eased the car to the curb in front of the house where she grew up she felt as if she had never been there before. The house had been painted and shutters added. To the side of the house was a new screened patio. The lawn was landscaped beautifully. Many of the old shrubs had been removed from the front of the house and in their places beds of bright flowers bloomed in profusion. The big window that her mother had always covered with heavy draperies to keep the house cool and dark was now shiny clean. Crisp cottage curtains framed the window and a row of green plants lined the sill.

Resentment, like bile, came up into her throat. Her father had never taken the slightest interest in the house while her mother was alive. It was true that her mother had definite likes and dislikes regarding the house and Lindy didn't always agree with them. For one thing her mother would have never allowed the thin curtains and the plants.

Lindy got out of the car and walked briskly to the door determined to get in and out in the shortest time possible. Her father and his bride — the word was bitter in her thoughts — had probably put her things in the attic, that is if they kept them at all.

It was insane to be ringing the doorbell of this house after so many years of bouncing in through the screened door, racing to the kitchen or up the stairs to her room, but there she stood, her finger prodding the button. When the door opened she was momentarily startled. She didn't know what she had expected. The woman had short gray hair cut in a wedge, a pleasant smiling face, and was wearing shorts and a T-shirt that said "SUPER MOM."

The smile left the woman's face, then returned quickly. "You're Lindy!" She opened the screened door. "I recognized you from your picture."

"Yes, I am," Lindy said flatly. "I've been away and . . . I left some of my things here. I'd like to get them."

"Of course. Come in. I'm Marilyn. Your father and I have been married for a year, now. I'm sorry we haven't met before."

"Well . . . If you'll tell me where my things are I'll try and get them out of your way."

"They're not in the way, dear. Come have a glass of tea. Charles will be here soon. He'll help you carry down anything you want to take with you. You're not in a hurry, are you? Wouldn't you like to look around the house? We have done a lot of work on it this past year. My land, I didn't know Charles could do so many things until we got started. He got so he could refinish woodwork and hang paper right along with the best of them." The woman was nervous. Somehow it made Lindy feel better to know this woman, who could inspire her father to do so much work on this house, was nervous of her.

The house didn't even remotely resemble the house she and her mother lived in, virtually alone, for so many years. The rooms were the same; it was the walls, the windows and the furniture that made it so different. The house was brighter, a cosy warm . . . home.

"Would you care for lemon with your tea?"

She looked at the woman standing hesitantly beside the big combination refrigerator-freezer and shook her head.

"Please don't bother. I want to get back to Galveston before the heavy traffic begins."

"If you're sure you don't have time . . ."

"I'm sure. If you'll tell me . . ."

"They're in your room," the woman said quickly. She walked past Lindy to the stairs. Lindy noticed she was quite short and a little plump. Not at all like her tall, very slender mother.

At the door of her old room the woman stood back and allowed Lindy to go in. She went through the door and stopped. It was like walking back into the years. Nothing had been changed. The shades were drawn, the room was shadowed, just as her mother insisted she keep it. Everything was in its place from the picture on the bedside table of her and her mother, taken when she was about ten years old, to the bulletin board with the high-school snapshots of her and Debbie. Shocked tears came to her eyes. She looked around, but the woman had backed out the door and closed it behind her.

Lindy stood for a long while. She realized, suddenly, she had been relieved to find the house changed, she hadn't wanted to see it as it was, remember all the lonely hours she had spent here not wanting to go out and leave her mother alone to sit with only the television to keep her company. For as long as she could remember, her mother had been weak, sickly. It had been Jean, Debbie's mom, who took them to the beach, was the Brownie Scout leader, came to watch her in the school plays.

It had all been her father's fault. She had

grown up knowing it was her and her mother against him. He was a "lusty" man, her mother had told her. It was more important to him to seek his own pleasure than to spend time at home with them. Lindy didn't want to remember these things. She had enough problems. Let her unhappy childhood stay dead.

She went out of the room and closed the door. She would get her things later. Much later, when she had a place of her own. It seemed her father and his wife had no immediate need for the room, and a few more weeks wouldn't matter.

The hall was empty when she reached it and she went quickly down the stairs. At the bottom she looked around for her father's wife. She came out of the kitchen, looking expectant, the friendly smile gone from her face.

"I'm out of time," Lindy said. "Will it inconvenience you if I leave my things for a while longer?" Lindy looked at the clock on the wall beside the woman's head as she spoke. It began to strike . . . a foreign sound in this house. Her mother couldn't stand the sound of a clock ticking, much less the sound of one striking. She remembered when her father had brought her a clock from Mexico . . . Her mother wouldn't allow her to keep it. Well . . . never mind that now. He knew she hated clocks.

"Inconvenience us? It's your room. Charles and I . . . we were hoping you would come visit us. I have two boys." She was talking fast again. Nervous. Some women were like that. She hesitated and when Lindy didn't comment about her boys she said again, "I have two boys and two grandsons."

"How nice. I really must go." The door behind her opened.

"Charles! Charles, look who came to see us!"

Lindy didn't want to turn around. Why had she come here? Why hadn't she grabbed up a few things and got out of here? She felt her feet moving and suddenly she was looking at him.

"Lindy? Lindy, girl . . ."

"Hello, Daddy."

She didn't think he had changed a great deal. His hair was a little grayer and he was thinner, but he did look younger . . . happier. She was surprised to see his eyes anxious. He didn't offer to touch her. They just stood there, separated by a lifetime of not even knowing one another.

"I hadn't heard that you were back from Alaska."

She nodded in silent answer.

"Where are you staying? You're welcome to . . ."

"I'm back with Jake." She almost choked on the words. "We have a house in Galveston." For a moment she wanted to blurt out that she had married the wrong person, just as he had so many years ago. It was unbearable to be standing there, being polite. Won't he quit looking at me, for heaven's sake?

"You've met Marilyn? We've . . ."

"She told me. I hope you're very happy. I must go. Jake . . ."

"Can't you stay a while?" He waved helplessly at the glasses Marilyn was holding on a tray. Were there tears in his eyes? No! Her father glad to see her? It was funny, but she didn't feel like laughing.

"No. No, thank you." She went to the door. "I'll call before I come back for my things. I'll try and get them soon. You may need the room for . . . your grandsons."

"There's no hurry." This came from Marilyn who put the tray on the table and was standing beside her father. Her head barely came above his shoulder. Why should she remember that her mother and father were about the same height? She nodded to the woman and glanced at her father. They were strangers. They had always been strangers.

" 'Bye, Daddy."

She went out and closed the door. She heard it open behind her and knew they were watching her go down the walk to her car, but she didn't turn around. It was a relief to get out into the cool air. The wind whipped her hair and dried the tears on her cheeks.

She drove the few blocks to Debbie's old home. To Jean's house. It had been here that she had known her happiest moments when she was a child. Twenty minutes later she sat on Jean's worn sofa and slowly, painfully, she started to sob. She hadn't mentioned her visit to her old home, or her father, but she had to get it out.

"He never cared about me." She said it like a heartbroken child.

"That isn't true," Jean said sternly. "Charlie never tried to come between you and your mother. He realized it would be like a tug of war with you in the middle and you would only be hurt more." She handed Lindy a wad of fresh tissue.

"Poor Mom. She led a dog's life with him."

"Your mother led the kind of life that made her happiest. It's time you realized she was happiest when she was miserable. I would never have said that to you while she was alive, but now . . . more than anything Marsha loved her martyrdom. I knew years before she went to the sanitarium that she was sick in mind."

"It was his fault! He drove her to it with his . . . playing around. He didn't love us. He never loved us. Mama loved him so much she couldn't stand to live with him year after year when he begrudged every minute he spent with us." Anger dried her eyes.

"Marsha never loved a living soul except herself." The bitter words shocked Lindy. She looked with astonishment at this woman who had been like a mother to her; who never said a bitter, unkind word about anyone. Jean saw the shocked look on her face and added, softly, "Lindy, I knew your mother before she married Charlie. She was a sheltered child, pretty, but sickly, and encouraged by her parents to be a clinging, whining woman."

Jean sat with her arms folded over her ample breast while Lindy searched her stern face. "She couldn't help it if she wasn't strong."

"That's true, but you must not blame Charlie for everything. He shouldn't have married her, but give him credit for staying married to her and taking care of her."

Why was Jean defending him? She knew how it was . . . how it had always been between her father and her mother.

"Oh, we had a roof over our heads and food to eat, but that's all we got from him. We would have been better off if he'd left us alone. It was his constant coming and going, his . . . women that drove Mama into a breakdown."

"Did you ever see your father with another woman? Did anyone else ever see Charlie out carousing with another woman? He didn't have time, for land's sake! He held down two jobs for years and years. He was a bartender at night. Marsha's medical bills were so big he had to have two jobs!"

"I can't believe that!" The shock and disbelief made her eyes huge as she stared at Jean. Why hadn't she been told this before? Jean read the question on her face.

"It was Charlie's idea. He thought it best to leave you to your mother. You were all she had and he didn't want to drive a wedge between you, but that didn't mean he didn't love you. He just didn't know how to go about showing it. Who do you think paid for the vacation trip to the Big Bend and to Carlsbad Caverns the year you and Debbie graduated? Charlie did. I didn't have the money for the trip. He didn't want you to know he arranged for me to take you and he certainly didn't want Marsha to know. She would have forbidden you to go."

"Why didn't you tell me? Why didn't Debbie tell me?"

"Debbie didn't know and I didn't think it was my place to interfere. Charlie had enough to contend with without me butting in." Jean was blunt as usual. "I thought after Marsha died you and Charlie would get to know each other, but you took off, right away, for Alaska. You should have told him you were going."

"He already had that other woman on the string," Lindy said stubbornly. "He was seeing her before Mama died. I know he was."

"Yes, he was. I admit it. He had known Marilyn for a long time. He was friends with her husband before he died. It was only a few months before Marsha died that he started seeing Marilyn in her home. He knew it was hopeless with Marsha and it had been a long time since he had had female companionship.

Why didn't you go to see him after the funeral and tell him you were taking the job in Alaska?"

"I had to leave right away. There were other reasons why I wanted to get out of Houston." Her voice was tight and Jean watched the expressions of confusion flit across her face.

"I know Charlie wasn't perfect, but he wasn't as bad as you were led to believe. I'm glad he's happy. He deserves it. Don't shut him and Marilyn out of your life, Lindy. They'll more than meet you halfway if you give them a chance." It stunned Lindy a little to think about it. The idea was too new, the story Jean told too incredible.

"I've got to go." She had to get away, to think, to try and absorb this new information about her parent. You can't change a lifetime of impressions about someone in an hour. "Thanks for letting me cry on your shoulder. I love you." She took Jean's hand and squeezed it hard. "You and Debbie have always been my real family."

Jean hugged her. "Don't let what happened between your mother and Charlie cloud your life with Jake. I know you love him . . . try and work things out."

The traffic took all her attention and she didn't have time to think until she was out on the freeway and then it was only fleeting snatches of thought. Daddy moonlighting the nights he spent away from home . . . her mother knew that, yet let her believe he was out with other women . . . why? Why destroy the love a little girl had for her father? Had daddy loved her after all? Mama was gone and Daddy was happy. She had to get her own life straightened out. Communicate, Debbie had said. Communicate? What could she say to Jake? Could she say I saw you on the couch with another woman? . . . it makes me sick to see you with Liz? . . . I don't believe you when you say you've not been sleeping around since you met me?

She had accused him of being like her father. Had she placed him in her father's role and she automatically assumed her mother's role? The thought caused her to press hard on the accelerator and the small car leaped ahead.

Chapter Fourteen

It was pouring down rain when Lindy neared the beach house; a warm, spring squall from the gulf spilled the rain in blinding sheets. She sat in the car and waited for the dark, water-laden cloud to pass before she dashed for the veranda. She slipped off her wet shoes and left them on a mat beside the door and went silently down the hall to her room. What she needed was a brandy, but she would have to settle for a cool shower.

Later Carlos knocked on the door to tell her that Jake would spend the night in the hospital. They had removed the cast and X-rayed his leg. A new cast would be applied in the morning and Carlos would drive in to bring him home. Lindy greeted the news with relief. She would not have to confront Jake tonight.

When Carlos left the next morning he was alone in the big Lincoln. Lindy had expected Liz to have her bags packed and ready to go back to Houston with him, but she didn't come out of her room until after he had left. She came to the kitchen, gave Lindy an insolent glance and asked Maria to fix her toast and coffee.

Lindy spoke up. "Fix it yourself. Maria's going back to her apartment to rest."

It must have been the tone of her voice that stopped Liz when she opened her mouth to reply, because she closed it again and went back into the office.

Lindy went to the blue and yellow living room and sat on the couch with her cup of coffee and tucked her long legs under her. The room was even prettier in the morning sun than it had been last night but it looked sad and empty. Just as Lindy felt sad and empty, unloved and frightened. Suddenly she desperately wanted to go home. But this was home! This beautiful house, on the sandy beach, surrounded by the swaying palms was home. But . . . it was a lonely, empty building and no one seemed to live here. It was ridiculous, but she longed to be back in Jean's house in Houston. Why didn't she go? She was a grown woman and could go if she wanted to go. She could get in the car and drive, lose herself in the millions of people out there, never see Jake again. It was absurd to sit in this house and wait for him. She could go and leave him to Liz or . . . she could stay . . . she had the right to stay. The perfect right.

The sun coming in through the window made a bright path on the blue carpet and she remembered the grueling cold of only a few weeks before. On sudden impulse she went to her room and put on her swimsuit. It was

Saturday. There were a few sailboats on the water and a few swimmers far down the beach. Armed with beach towels, lotion, sunglasses and a paperback novel, she slipped her feet into scuffs, because of the remembered cockleburs, and went down the path to the water.

Her mind wandered to Jake as she walked, and she was annoyed at herself. Why should she feel almost guilty because she could see the water, the white sand, could go anyplace she wanted to go without being led? His blindness was only temporary!

She tried to empty her mind of thought as she lay in the warm sunshine, but words kept echoing in her head. Communicate . . . talk it out . . . you've got to decide if you can forgive him. She dozed, woke and applied more lotion, dozed again, then decided to try the novel. She knew it would be foolhardy to fall asleep in the sun. After a time she threw the book down in exasperation — it was no good, she just couldn't concentrate. Giving up, she packed her things and trudged back to the house.

Lindy peeled off her swimsuit and after a quick shower stretched out on the bed. Jake would surely be back from the hospital by now. She looked at her watch and promised herself she would go to his room in a couple of hours for the showdown Debbie suggested. She didn't want to take any more time to think about what she wanted to say to him. She was tired of thinking. She wanted to get it over. Find out exactly where she stood. If he refused to send Liz packing, she would leave. But . . . she would do what she had to do. It was stupid to worry about being alone, about her future, without Jake. She would survive. She was convinced that she was a survivor . . . like Jake. She would swallow her pride one more time and if it didn't work out . . . well . . . Tears, that she shed so easily, wet the pillow beneath her cheek.

She woke up shortly before seven, was dressed and out on the veranda by seven-thirty. Liz and Jake were there, Jake sitting with his leg propped up on an ottoman. A partly filled ashtray with a cigarette still burning was on the table beside him. Lindy hesitated, tempted to go back into the house and return later to talk to Jake. Liz spoke to her before she could make up her mind.

"Did you have a good sleep? Jake asked me to look in on you when dinner was ready, but you were sleeping so soundly I didn't want to disturb you."

Jake held out his hand to her. Somehow she couldn't bear to make contact with him in front of Liz.

"You had better have something to eat." He let his hand drop back down to the arm of the chair and she could see his fingers gripping it as if it were a weapon. "I'll ask Carlos to fix a plate of food for you. Just slip it into the microwave for a minute to warm it up."

"How is your leg?"

"It's all right as long as I don't move it around too much."

"After I eat I want to talk with you. Alone." She shot a glance at Liz who smiled a private, tight smile and raised her brows. The gesture angered her and she snapped, "If you can spare the time, that is."

"Of course I have the time. Liz has work to do anyway. I'll wait for you here."

She hated to hear that name on his lips and she hated herself for allowing Liz to see that she hated it. She took her time eating, trying not to plan on what she would say to Jake. It had to be open, spontaneous, to be honest. That's what Debbie said. Keep an open mind, then decide if you can forgive him.

It was dusk, that time between daylight and dark that the poets write about. One soft lamp was burning as she passed through the living room. Liz was ahead of her, having come from the hall as she came from the kitchen. She hesitated, tempted to wait until Liz went back to the office, but the desire to get the talk over with was greater than her wish to avoid Liz and so she walked swiftly to the open door.

Liz was standing behind Jake, her palm against his cheek. He reached for her hand and pulled her toward him.

"Sweetheart," he said huskily. "Sweetheart, she won't be back for a while. Come here. God,

I can't wait to see you!" He drew the unresisting Liz down on his lap.

Lindy gaped, unable to utter a sound, incapable of accepting what she was seeing. The pain was fresh, sharp and hurt like hell! Shaken to the core she turned and fled down the hall to her room and went straight to the bed. She didn't cry. She didn't think about what she had seen. Strangely she felt relief. Now, at last, she knew for sure! It was like sitting on the edge of a cold pool wanting to plunge in and yet not wanting to. Someone comes along and pushes you and you're glad. She lay there for a long time, staring at the ceiling, wondering if she should call Debbie. She didn't want to talk to anyone right now, but it was a comfort to know she could call if she wanted to. Debbie would come if she called. Debbie would come and get her tomorrow.

She got up and turned the lock on the door, undressed and got into bed. Almost at once a strange sensation began seeping rapidly through her mind, a fuzziness, a distant humming noise sounded in her ears, soothing her, relaxing her. She seemed to float upward, her arms and legs losing their solidity, the tense cords that held her back so rigid releasing, and she lay in limbo.

The knob on the door turned. She didn't care.

"Lindy." Jake's voice was soft. "Are you all right? Open the door. I thought you wanted to talk."

"I've changed my mind," she said tiredly. An endless sigh shook her entire body. It had been an unbearable day. The most unbearable day of her life. The pain and the pressure seemed endless.

"Why did you lock the door?" He was angry. So what? His anger didn't matter to her anymore.

"Go away, Jake. I want to sleep."

"What the hell is the matter with you? Are you sick? Did you get too much sun?"

"Nothing's the matter. I just want to sleep."

Silence and then his voice loud and angry.

"Sleep then, damn you!"

She did. It was strange, but even without the sleeping pills her anguished mind sought refuge in sleep. Curled up in a ball, her hand beneath her cheek, she slept soundly. Later she was to wonder if at that time her mind was slipping away from her.

Suddenly she was awakened. Her eyes sprang open and soon adjusted to the moonlit room. She heard again the soft thump on the carpet that had awakened her. She wasn't frightened. She lay perfectly still, listening, waiting. Before she saw the figure of the man limp around the end of the bed she knew that Jake was in her room and that it was the hard cast on his leg that had made the thumping sound.

She lay motionless and watched his every move. He still had on his clothes as if he had not been to bed. He came to stand beside her, so close she could have touched him had she stretched out her fingers. Breathlessly she watched as his hand came out and slowly, as if not to wake her, touch her hair; then fingertips light as air, trailed across her forehead. The back of his hand rested for an instant against her cheek. She heard a sound come from him. It was a sigh, a groan or a sharp expulsion of air. She couldn't tell which. With wide and curious eyes she watched him limp back around the bed and out of sight. The soft click of the door told her she was alone.

She drifted off to sleep again and when morning came the scene that had occurred in the middle of the night was as vague in her memory as a dream.

It was dawn when she opened her dry and burning eyes. The emotional upheaval of the night before had left her with an aching head and a listless body. She showered and slipped into a pair of white slacks and a red-and-white-striped sleeveless top. After giving her hair a quick brush she padded barefoot out to the kitchen, sure it was far too early for anyone to be about.

Someone had been there before her and the aroma of freshly perked coffee filled the room. Taking a mug from the shelf she helped herself to the coffee and went back through the main room to the veranda where she could sit and look out over the water and wait until time to call Debbie.

She was about to sit down in a lounge chair when Jake's voice startled her.

"Morning." It was a low, calm voice, but it broke the tranquil silence. Her nerves were jumpy and her hand shook, spilling some of the hot coffee on her bare feet.

"Oh, oh . . ." The sound was out before she could suppress it.

"What's the matter?"

"Nothing. I just spilled a little coffee." She set the cup on the table not knowing if she should go or stay.

"Sit down and drink your coffee."

She glanced at him. His face was turned away from her as if he was looking out over the water. His hearing had sharpened since his blindness and he was waiting for the creak of the wicker chair.

She sat down and let her curious eyes wander over him. This man, her husband, was hard to understand. There were times when she felt she didn't know him at all. He knew she had loved him before. Did he expect her to love him again? To sweep all his indiscretions into a corner like so much dust? She could never love him as she once loved him — blindly, wholeheartedly, consumingly. What woman with pride and self-esteem and memory could?

Jake had just come from the shower. His

hair as well as the cast on his leg was wet. He was wearing walking shorts and his muscled chest and shoulders were bare. The sunglasses helped to hide the expression on his face, but she did see a grimace when he reached a finger down to work it around the top of the cast that came almost to his knee. The leg was propped on a stool and the part of his foot not covered with the cast was almost as white as the plaster. Lindy guessed that he had been careless and allowed water to splash around the top of the cast and an itch had developed.

Slowly she shifted her gaze away from him and the world looked steady again. She drew air into her lungs in great gulps in order to stop her trembling so she could hold her coffee cup. Her heart thumped in her throat when he spoke.

"You didn't come back last night."

"I came," she said aloud and to herself . . . I came . . . I saw . . ."

"I waited and you didn't come."

"I came," she repeated. "You were busy." Her lips trembled at the memory. It was too soon to be completely indifferent although she managed to say indifferently, "You were very busy."

"Why didn't you ask me how long I would be . . . busy?"

She was momentarily startled at the question. "I didn't even consider asking you that!"

He turned toward her, his hand spread in a gesture of futility.

"What now? Are you leaving me again?"

Quite simply she answered, "Yes."

His face was turned in her direction. He looked tired, haggard: there were deep creases on each side of his mouth. She looked searchingly at him for a long moment. The shock was over. She was able to speak calmly.

"You don't need me, Jake. With all you've got you don't need me."

He took a quivering breath. "Wedding vows don't mean much to you, do they?"

Anger brought her to her feet. "You . . . can say that to me?"

"You loved me once."

"Yes, I did," she admitted. "But that was . . . before . . . "

"Before what?"

"You know the 'before what' I'm talking about. I don't have to spell it out for you." She crossed over to the door.

"Just a minute. We haven't finished this conversation." She could hear Jake getting clumsily to his feet.

"It's finished. The conversation is finished. We're finished." Feeling the trembling weakness of reaction in her knees and the overwhelming desire to get away from him, she headed, unsteadily, for her bedroom.

On reaching the hall her unsteady legs picked up speed and she was almost running.

A door opened and she stood stockstill, staring transfixed, her mouth open in shocking surprise, acute humiliation causing her face to flood with color.

Liz was coming out of Jake's room and through the open door she could see the rumpled bed and the filmy black robe lying on it. The bit of black sheer that covered Liz probably served as an excuse for a nightgown and it revealed most all of her as she stretched and yawned.

Lindy wanted to pass on, but her legs refused to move. Goddamn them! Goddamn them both to hell! The voice inside her shouted her desire to kill them . . . to run . . . to not believe what she was seeing.

Jake came into the hall and Liz called to him.

"Shall we have our coffee now, Jake?" She stifled a yawn.

Jake didn't answer for a moment and Lindy found life in her legs and moved fast toward her bedroom feeling physically sick.

"Get dressed, Liz, and come to the office." There was a strange quality in his voice. "Lindy, go get Carlos." It was a command. With his hand on the wall he walked as rapidly as his injured leg would allow to the small office.

Liz looked as smug as a cat who had just swallowed a canary and her soft quivering laughter sent Lindy's temper climbing. She hurried by her and came face to face with Jake. Her lips curled in disgust and her face was a mask of contempt.

Jake's hand shot out and grabbed her by the forearm. The action surprised her so much she took several backward steps to regain her balance.

"Don't leave this house!" Jake was gripped with a consuming rage. Lindy almost recoiled from the cold fury on his face.

"Get your hands off me!" Her voice was so hard she scarcely recognized it as her own. "Don't touch me . . . ever!" She jerked away from him and went quickly toward the kitchen.

She leaned on the counter. Her head felt light and her vision blurred. She turned the cold water into the sink and held both wrists under the stream. The last few minutes had upset her more than she thought possible. How long would it go on? How much more would she be able to take? Each incident hurt more than the one before it. She turned off the water, dried her hands and dialed Debbie's number. She let the phone ring ten times before she hung up the receiver and went to find Carlos.

Refusing to go back into the house after she had given Carlos the message, Lindy found a shady spot under a palm tree and sat down on the grass and rested her back against the sturdy trunk. She had never felt so alone in all her life and wished desperately she had been able to reach Debbie. She looked at her watch. She would wait a half hour and call again.

A worried-looking Carlos came to tell her *Señor* Jake wanted her to come into the house.

"What does he want?" she asked bluntly.

"He going to Houston, *señora,* and want to say something before he go."

Lindy got to her feet and followed him across the yard. Jake was standing on the drive. He had changed into sports shirt and light trousers. He was leaning against the car, his face was toward her as she approached.

She looked directly at him for if her plans worked this could be the last time she would see him. He was handsome, no use to deny that. She had thought she could live with the "peaks" and endure the "valleys," but she couldn't. No use to deny that, either.

He spoke immediately. "I'm going to Houston." He waited and she said nothing, so he continued. "Carlos will drive me. We want to be sure you will stay here with Maria. Carlos is worried she may go into labor and not have anyone with her."

The bottom fell out of Lindy's plans. She looked at Carlos's worried face and back to Jake. "Your *friend* will be here."

"Liz is going with me."

"I see."

243

"I'm sure you do." No mistaking the sarcasm.

"How long will you be gone?"

"Until this afternoon."

"I'll stay while you're gone."

Carlos perked up and smiled his usual toothy smile.

"*Gracias, señora.* I not like to leave her, you know, she will be so scared when the baby come. Maybe it won't be this day, maybe next day and Carlos will be here to take care of her."

"Why can't your . . . friend take you and let Carlos stay with his wife?" She spoke in the measured tone of a woman who knew her life with this man was over.

Jake answered in the same tone. "Because my . . . friend is leaving and not coming back. Carlos will take me to the clinic and bring me back. After that you can do as you damn well please."

She stared at him. She could see her image reflected in his dark glasses. There seemed nothing else to say.

Liz came out of the house carrying her cases. She hadn't taken her usual time with her appearance. Her hair was pulled back from a makeup-free face, she had pulled on jeans and a knit top. Her feet were thrust into exercise sandals. She dropped her cases at the rear of the car, then got in and sat huddled in the corner of the back seat. Lindy had never seen her other than arrogant and self-assured and she was shocked into confusion. Something very strange was going on, but what it was she couldn't fathom. Jake's voice broke into her perplexing thoughts.

"Find Maria and assure her she won't be left alone. You'll be all right here. Take care of yourself." He started giving his orders in a tense, clipped voice. It softened on the last request and he would have touched her arm but she sidestepped and went up the steps to the veranda.

Inside the screened porch she turned and looked at the group on the drive. Jake had eased himself into the right front seat. His face was turned toward where she was standing and she could see a sad and serious look on his face that left her puzzled.

Maria came to stand beside her. She waved to Carlos and he returned her wave. She stood silently and watched the car until it was out of sight.

"I hope baby not come today." Maria's big brown eyes were solemn. "I need Carlos when he come."

Compassion for this young girl flooded her. It had been a million years since she had been this young and this in love.

"Don't worry. They'll be back in a few hours. You feel all right?"

"I don't feel no different, *señora*."

"Come and sit down. I'll make us some fresh coffee."

"I make you coffee, *señora*. You the lady. I the servant."

"Lady? Servant? Who said so?"

Maria blinked her eyes and smilingly shook her head. "You so different from the *señorita*. Carlos and I not stay with the *señor* if she *Señorita* Williamson. I glad she go and not come back."

Maria sat in the kitchen chair, a soft pillow nestled in the small of her back. Lindy set the toaster on the table and added butter and jam. It soothed her nerves to be doing something.

"Maria, you can't be sure Liz won't be back. She won't be back today, but she'll be back soon."

"I don't think so. Carlos say the *señor* very, very angry. He call office and say write the *señorita* a check. She don't work for him. The *señorita* cry and say she sorry, but the *señor* say she cost him too much and he not want to put eyes on her again."

Lindy was stunned into silence. Jake had fired Liz? Slept with her the night before and fired her in the morning? Maybe he planned to set her up in an apartment . . . but no, if that was the case Liz wouldn't have cried and she would have been more arrogant than ever this morning. Jake was a puzzle. Her head ached from all the confused thoughts that floated through it and she wished with all her heart that she had never set eyes on Jake Williamson.

Chapter Fifteen

After a light lunch Maria lay down to rest and Lindy fixed herself an iced drink and went out on the veranda. She settled in a lounge chair and tried to sort out the confusing mass of information Maria had given her. After a while she grew tired of trying to figure out the complex person she was married to and allowed her mind to go blank.

A car came into the drive and moved slowly past the garages toward the house. Lindy sat up in the chair, her heart quickening. Could Jake be back so soon? No . . . it was a black car. The man behind the wheel had on a white Stetson hat. The car stopped. A tall familiar figure unfolded itself and got out.

She sprang to her feet and ran down the steps. She was almost blinded by tears by the time she reached him and threw her arms around his waist and buried her face on his broad chest. Sobs shook her slim body and she cried uncontrollably, her tears making wet patches on his shirt.

"Honey! What's the matter?" Buck's voice was anxious.

"Everything!" The word came out between sobs.

"Has something happened to Jake?"

"Jake's all right," Lindy said when she could catch her breath. She stepped away from Buck and saw a pretty dark-haired girl with a small boy clinging to each of her hands. The boys were wide-eyed and silent, the girl's face showed questioning concern. Her resemblance to Jake was unmistakable.

"I'm sorry." They were weak words, but all she could think of in defense of her actions.

"That's okay, honey. It isn't every day I have a pretty girl cry on my shoulder." Buck put his arm out and drew the little group closer to him. "This is Mary Ellen and Mack and Pete. Boys, this is your Uncle Jake's wife."

Mary Ellen embraced her. "Did we come at a bad time?"

"I'm sorry I frightened you. I guess it was seeing Buck again. He was such a pillar of strength in Alaska. Jake has gone to Houston to have the doctor take a look at his leg. I suspect he's developed an itch under the cast." She looked down at the two pair of blue eyes staring up at her. "I'm glad to meet you, boys."

"Are you crying cause you're having a baby?"

Of all the things a child could have said this was the most astonishing and Lindy's lips parted on an involuntary breath. On this unguarded moment her unconscious fear had found voice.

"Pete!" Mary Ellen scolded with her eyes as well as her voice.

"Uncle Jake said he was going to get a baby as soon as he got back. So . . ." Pete stammered, then halted.

"No, to your question, Pete." Lindy found her voice. "I was crying because it was so good to see Buck again."

Mack turned a serious little face to her. "But . . . Buck is goin' to marry us." His eyes went from Lindy to Buck. "Pete and I are goin' to have a daddy and Buck is it."

Lindy leaned down and hugged him. "You and Pete will have the best daddy in the whole world."

"Then . . . you won't cry no more?"

"I won't. I promise."

Buck had his arm around Mary Ellen and he looked stupidly, gloriously happy.

"They're perfect for you, Buck." Lindy was never more sincere about anything in her life. "And to steal a cliché from you . . . you look like you had the world by the tail going down hill backward!"

Buck laughed. "Well, darned if I don't!" He hugged Mary Ellen tighter. "Who wouldn't be happy as a ringtailed bobcat with a woman like this and two Texas mule skinners?"

"What's a ringtailed bobcat?" This from Pete.

"What's a Texas muleskinner?" yelled Mack.

Mary Ellen detached herself from Buck's arms. "Okay, Buck." Her smile was indulgent. "You started it. You explain."

"He can explain in the house while I make

249

a cool drink," Lindy said and led the way onto the veranda.

In the kitchen she left Mary Ellen to add ice to the lemonade while she made a hurried trip to check on Maria, after explaining Maria's condition.

"That will interest Pete." Mary Ellen laughed. "Right now he has an obsession about babies. He keeps mentioning it to Buck. Honestly, it's embarrassing!"

"Buck is a real gem. I don't know what I'd have done without him in Fairbanks. He risked his life to save Jake. Did he tell you that?"

"He told me something about it, but said you did more." Lindy dismissed the remark with a shrug. "Shall we take the drinks to the boys?"

Later, while Mary Ellen and the boys toured the house and the grounds, Buck questioned Lindy about Jake.

"He's doing all right. He's been in to the hospital and had a new cast put on his leg." She decided to change the subject and said the first thing that came to mind. "I was disappointed when you didn't meet us at the airport."

"I'm sorry about that. I phoned Mary Ellen and she seemed to be so glad to hear from me that I hightailed it down there." He grinned sheepishly. "Did Don keep you waiting?"

"Don?" Lindy echoed. "Liz met us." She despised saying the name.

"Don was to meet you so Carlos could stay with Maria."

"Liz said you made the arrangements for her to meet us and that you would pick her up here in a few days." She looked away from him. The memory was too painful, and she must not let herself cry again.

"Liz came here with you?"

"Yes. She went back to Houston this morning with Jake."

Buck looked out over the gulf, his eyes narrowed in that particular way of his. "You haven't been happy, have you, honey?"

"No." She dropped her eyes and stared at her hands. "I have never been so miserable in my life."

"But . . . you love him."

Her shoulders straightened defiantly. "No . . . yes . . . No! I detest what he is!" she protested incredulously, resentful of Buck's reception when he looked at her.

"Why did you marry him then?" Buck's gaze held hers for a moment longer, grew speculative, then pensive.

She was so damn vulnerable, she realized with a pang. Weak, and vulnerable and pathetically unsure of herself. The complexities of Jake's character forced her to denounce her feelings for him. She thought for a moment before answering, as if she had never thought seriously about it before.

"I don't know." Her lips trembled. "I knew it was the wrong thing to do when I did it. But . . . Jake is so overwhelming, so determined. He's stronger than I, Buck. And not just physically. I mean he has a stronger personality and I thought he needed me. But Jake doesn't need anyone. Jake is a complete unit himself, and . . ." She stopped abruptly, not really knowing how to explain. After a moment she continued. "I'm leaving him. I'd just as soon Mary Ellen didn't know just yet."

Buck waited a while before he said, "Don't do anything hasty. Jake loves you. That man went through hell when you left him before. You understand it's not for me to be telling you what to do, but I'd swear on my daddy's Bible that he loves you."

"Maybe Jake does love me, in his own way, but it's not the way I want to be loved. I've caught him in situations that I just can't forgive. And to let that woman come to this house . . . I'm just not all that liberated, Buck." Try as she might she couldn't keep the tears from rolling down her cheeks. They sat silently. Finally, she regained her composure and said, "When is the wedding?"

His dark eyes took on a glow. "In exactly forty-eight hours."

"Great! Where will you live?"

"I've rented a house a mile down the beach. Mary Ellen and the boys will stay there until I move in with them." He grinned happily.

Two bundles of energy burst from the house and threw themselves on Buck. "Ain't we goin' swimmin', Buck?"

Buck got to his feet holding a small wiggling boy under each arm. He took them to the door and set them on their feet. "Out to the car, cowboys. Your mom and I will be out in a minute and we'll go home. Mind, now, or I'll tan your hides!"

The boys bounded down the steps. Mary Ellen looked fondly after them and gazed lovingly at Buck. "You're just what they need."

"And you, little bird?" He put his arms around her.

"Me, too." She wrapped her arms around him.

Lindy watched them leave. They were already a united family, something she had never known. When the car turned the drive and was out of sight, she went back into the house.

By evening Maria was convinced the baby would not arrive that day. Lindy was glad for her company. They sat in companionable silence, Maria knitting and Lindy working on her needlepoint. It was just getting dark when they heard the small blast of the horn.

"That Carlos!" Maria jumped up, clutching her knitting to her full breast, and hurried to the door and down the steps.

Lindy sat as if paralyzed. Damn! It was too late to call Debbie. The dreaded moment had come and she would have to face Jake once again. The lamps were lit in the attractive room and their soft glow fell on her worried face. Would Liz be with him? Had Maria misunderstood Carlos and Jake had not fired her after all? Lindy stood in the middle of the room, waiting. Her eyes looked like sapphires, dark and troubled.

She heard Jake call teasingly to Maria. She heard Carlos laugh. The screen door slammed and Jake was standing in the doorway. The first thing she noticed was that his sunglasses were different. They were light in color and she could see his eyes through the lens. She looked behind him. He was alone. He came slowly into the room holding his hand in front of him.

Lindy trembled violently as she watched him. "Do you need help?" She asked the question to let him know she was in the room.

He came to the back of the couch. "No. I can find my way."

His eyes were on her and she shivered. She wished he wouldn't face her. She felt uncomfortable knowing he couldn't see.

"Did they change your cast again?" She wondered how long she could stand there making polite conversation. Damn you, if only I could bring you the pain and the bitterness you've brought to me. Why didn't she say it? Why did she have to say something as civilized as "Did they change your cast?"

"Yes." He stood there leaning heavily on the back of the couch as if to relieve his leg of the burden of his weight. "What did you do today?"

The question surprised her. He didn't really care what she did today . . . he was the one now who was making the polite conversation. What would he say if she told him she had been out sleeping around? She didn't say any of the things she was thinking.

"Buck was here today with your sister."

"Mary Ellen was here?"

"Buck is going to marry her. He's rented a house about a mile down the beach."

Jake was pleased. His face relaxed and he almost smiled. "They'll be perfect together. What did you think of Mary Ellen?"

She answered truthfully. "I liked her. The boys, too."

Now he did smile. "What did the monsters think about Buck?"

"They liked him. Buck will be a good father." Lindy started to edge toward the door. "She left a number if you want to call her."

"Come here for a minute." He held out his hand.

She stopped, confused. Could he have known she was trying to leave the room?

"What do you want?" Her tone held a shade of desperation.

"Please." His expression was grave, his voice soft.

She looked at the hand he held out to her.

The gold wedding band she had given him shone brightly on his brown finger. She seemed to be drawn to that hand, so she went to him. He grasped her hand tightly and pulled her to him. She tried to pull away, but his fingers closed tightly around her wrist and brought it up against his lips. He kissed the soft skin.

"Did you mean what you said this morning about leaving me?"

Her lower lip quivered and she refused to look at him. "Yes!"

"Sweetheart!" His embrace enfolded her, bringing her tight against him. "Sweetheart, don't go! Give it a little more time." He trembled violently and his arms crushed her so close she could scarcely breathe. Her mind whirled giddily and she tried to push herself away from him.

"Don't!" Her words were a whisper coming from her tight throat.

He found her mouth and kissed her hungrily. Her lips already parted in protest, and his unexpected assault found no opposition. The weight of his muscular thighs pushing her back against the back of the couch was in itself a potent intoxicant, but it was his mouth that wrought the most damage, invading and possessing the moistness of hers. She was invaded by that old familiar feeling of weakness in her thighs as his fingers probed beneath her shirt, unrestrained in their caresses.

His withdrawal was as unexpected as his assault. One moment his mouth was on hers, devastating it, moving sensually, causing all the old familiar feelings to surface. The next moment he had lifted his head.

"Don't you love me enough?" The words were wrung from him.

"No! Not *that* much!"

With all her strength she tore herself from his arms and ran from the room. She felt helpless against the storm of emotion he had aroused inside her, dazed by her response to his arrogant assault. It was humiliating to know that he only had to touch her, kiss her, to tear down every defense she built against him. She had to get away from him. He could make her forget all that had happened in the past, and all that would happen in the future.

She leaned on the closed door of her room. Dear Jesus! Would this nightmare never be over? She had to leave this house tonight, or she might never be able to leave it at all. She took her overnight case from the shelf and started filling it with only the absolute necessities. In ten minutes she was ready to leave the room.

It was then her mind paused to grapple with the problem of transportation. What now? She couldn't ask Debbie to drive down here this late at night. The only other person she knew was Buck. She fished in her pocket for the folded paper which she had intended to give to Jake. Glancing at it she quickly dialed the number.

Mary Ellen answered the phone and she asked to speak to Buck.

"Hi, honey. What's the problem. Jake not home yet?"

"I hate to ask you to leave Mary Ellen and the boys, Buck, but will you come over and give me a ride into town? It's terribly important to me that I go tonight." Her voice shook in spite of her desperate attempt to control it.

"Of course I will, honey. Is there somewhere special you want to go?"

"To a hotel." She was losing her courage and her voice showed it.

For a short moment there was silence at the other end of the line. "If you're sure that's what you want to do I'll be there in ten minutes."

"I'll wait for you out by the garages."

"Okay. See you soon."

Lindy looked at her watch and paced the floor. The time went slowly, but it went by. She picked up her case and left the room.

Jake was standing in almost the same spot as when she left him. He had a drink in his hand. She walked softly, hoping to slip by without him knowing she was there.

"Lindy." His voice stopped her.

She halted momentarily, then moved on toward the door.

"There's no need for you to sneak out. I won't force myself on you." There was cold sarcasm in his tone.

She looked at him and his blue-green eyes held her frozen gaze with the expertise of the snake with the rabbit, and her heart seemed to choke her with her sudden realization.

"You can . . . see!"

"I'll never ask you to come back." He overrode her statement cruelly and limped to the table and set his glass down. There was a kind of desperation in his jerky movements. "Go! You think you know so God-awful much. Your problem is that you never cared enough to get to the bottom of anything that concerns me." He shouted the last words and she was sure that had he still had the glass in his hand he would have thrown it at her.

She saw the flash of headlights on the drive and turned.

"Good-bye, Jake."

"Lindy, wait. Where are you going?"

She ran down the steps as Buck's car turned into the drive. The headlights, arching in the darkness, found her and pulled to a stop beside her. The interior light came on when she opened the door and she saw Mary Ellen behind the wheel. Indecision . . . she stepped back, confused. Her frightened eyes saw Jake framed in the veranda doorway.

"Get in the car," Mary Ellen urged gently.

She got in and held the small overnight case on her lap. Her nerves were a screaming mass of loose ends that threatened to strangle her at any moment. Mary Ellen eased the big car back down the drive and out onto the highway.

Still unable to relax even the slightest bit, Lindy sat ramrod stiff as the car picked up speed. Mary Ellen hadn't said another word. Presently she pulled the car into the parking area of a closed supermarket, shut down the motor and turned off the lights.

Words fell from Lindy's mouth like rain. They tumbled over each other in their effort to find release. "Take me to a hotel. Please, I know what I'm doing. Tomorrow I'm going to Houston and find an apartment. I couldn't ask Carlos to take me and it's too late for me to ask my friend, Debbie, to come get me. The only other person I could think of was Buck. I'm sorry to get you involved in this."

"I wanted a chance to talk to you. It was Buck's idea for me to come for you. He's worried about you and Jake."

"The last thing I want to do is to worry anyone and especially you and Buck. This is your happiest time. All I can say is that I'm sorry, Mary Ellen." Her voice was hoarse and unnatural and she hugged the case tightly to her breast as if to stop the pounding of her heart.

"It's all right," Mary Ellen said gently. "I'm glad you called us. I don't need to tell you that I love my brother very much. He's all the family I've ever had. Do you love him?" The question was asked earnestly, abruptly, and

Mary Ellen leaned toward her to peer into her face.

Lindy waited a while before answering. She swallowed several times to get rid of the aching lump in her throat. "What is love? Is love wanting to go to bed with someone? Or . . . mutual respect, trust, blind faith that the person you love will never let you down, be unfaithful to you?" Looking out the window into the darkness, she stifled a sob.

"Do you?" Mary Ellen insisted. "It's yes or no. You love him or you don't."

"I don't know if I do or not!" The words were blurted out angrily. "I'm human. I like what he does to me, but I hate what he is on the inside!"

Mary Ellen settled back in the seat. "Somehow I think you do love him." She waited for Lindy to find a tissue and blow her nose. "He loves you. You have no idea how much Jake loves you and how badly he wants you to love him in return." She made this statement simply and honestly.

"I think Jake is fond of me in his own way. I said as much to Buck this afternoon. But it isn't the way I want to be loved. I want to be everything to my husband — wife, lover, friend, companion. I won't share him! I lived with a heartbroken mother. My father had many affairs with other women." Oh, Jesus! What was she saying? She didn't even know if that was true anymore.

"Jake told me something about your home life. He came to see me after you left him. He was heart-sick! He almost killed himself drinking and messing around in some of the lowest dives in Mexico City. After a while he thought he could build a life without you and he tried. He took on some very dangerous work in revolutionary countries. He wanted the big money, but he seemed to want the risk, too."

She paused to give Lindy time to take in the meaning of her words. "When he came back to Mexico City he seemed to have gotten himself together. He had made up his mind what he was going to do. He said life wasn't worth living without you and that he was coming home and he was going to buy the house you had dreamed of having and he was going to Alaska to get you."

"He broke my heart once!"

"You broke his," Mary Ellen said simply.

"You can't know how it was. A girl came to our apartment and said that Jake had made her pregnant. I tried to believe him when he denied it, but the doubt was always there."

"And you believed a stranger over a man who had never given you reason to doubt him before?"

"Before, no. Afterward, yes. More than doubt. Proof. I saw him on our own couch with Liz. Since we've been here in Galveston . . . they've been together!" The memory was so painful she could hardly speak of it.

"Does Jake know you know about this?" Mary Ellen had a disbelieving expression on her face.

"He knows."

"I can't believe Jake would do that. It goes against everything that I know about him." The dogged look of disbelief was still in her eyes. "Well . . . what does he say?"

"We never talk about it. He thinks I should trust him. He said if I loved him enough I would trust him." The pain of thinking about it was tearing through her again and a small moan escaped her.

Mary Ellen was thoughtful. "He doesn't explain his actions." It was a statement accompanied by a sad shake of her head. "Let me tell you something about Jake's early life. You think you had it rough? You had at least one parent that loved you. Jake had none. Our father died when we were very young and our mother was the type of woman who should never have had children. She was little and pretty and Jake loved her dearly, but there was something about him that made her actually . . . dislike him. He never did anything that pleased her. Any little thing that went wrong, Jake was blamed for it. If a window was broken out in the neighborhood she accused him whether anyone else thought he was guilty or not. If she misplaced money, he took it. She never took his word for anything.

Always she believed the worst of him. Even when she was ill, she accused him of not caring if she died. He developed an attitude that he would explain himself to no one. He knew she didn't love him, because she didn't trust him, have any confidence in him. That's a terrible burden for a small boy to carry. I realize it more now that I have boys of my own. Mary Ellen paused and wiped her eyes. "I understand my brother and I'll never believe in a million years that he was unfaithful to you."

"I saw him with my own eyes!"

"I know you think you saw . . . you did see . . . but talk to him about it. I know he loves you! Ask him to explain. Please, Lindy . . . talk to him."

Talk to him. It was what Debbie urged her to do. She sat silently, thinking.

"Tell him to straighten up or you'll knock his damned head off!" The unruffled Mary Ellen was now ruffled and Lindy was strangely calm.

How could Jake explain away Liz on his lap . . . Liz furnishing the house . . . Liz in his bedroom? Should she go back and open old wounds? Old wounds? Brand new wounds! Her hair lay damp and matted around her face, and for what seemed the thousandth time that night she wiped her eyes and her nose.

Mary Ellen took Lindy's silence for an answer and started the car. She didn't speak. She turned in the direction of the beach house.

"I'm scared," Lindy blurted suddenly. "I don't know what to say to him. I don't want to be hurt!"

"Life is full of hurts, Lindy. How do you know when you are happy if you have nothing to compare it with? It's a competitive world. Fight for what you want."

The car turned into the drive and stopped in front of the veranda steps.

"Go on," Mary Ellen said gently. "I'll come back if you call me."

Lindy reached over, kissed her on the cheek and got out of the car.

Chapter Sixteen

The soft lights were on in the living room and reached out onto the veranda where she stood. The only sound she heard was the pounding of the surf on the sand beach and the wind stirring the fronds of the palm trees. The sound of Mary Ellen's car had been lost to her for several minutes.

Her life played across the screen of her mind like a movie. Suddenly everything was clear. The guilt she felt for wanting to love her father in spite of his so-called "adulterous" behavior had almost turned that love to hate. The love-hate relationship had carried over into her marriage with Jake. Unconsciously she had cast him in her father's role and herself in the role of the martyred, repressed wife. Lindy felt a surge of rebellion! She would not walk in anyone's footsteps but her own.

She placed one foot in front of the other one until she stood in the middle of the living room. And then, almost before she knew it, she was in the hall. The door to Jake's room was open and the light made a path out onto the carpet. This was the turning point in her life. She was well aware of the importance of the moment. Without hesitation she moved to the door.

Jake lay on the bed with pillows propped behind his head. Only brief shorts covered his near-naked body that looked golden brown against the white sheets.

She struggled against the grayness that engulfed her and through the ringing in her ears she heard him say, "Did you forget something?"

Her lips were dry and she put out her tongue to moisten them. She shook her head to free herself from the daze and suddenly her mind was clear.

She walked into the room and stood looking down at him. Rage such as she never knew existed boiled up inside her. She forced her clenched fists to stay at her sides to keep them from striking him. Words she never thought of saying burst from her lips. "If you ever bring that bitch into my house again I'll knock your damn head off! I've put up with all I'm going to take from you, Jake Williamson!"

Her voice rose shrilly and to her astonishment she found herself shouting. "I've put up with your flirting, your playing around, but when you let that . . . woman come into *my* house you pushed me too far!" Her finger came out and jabbed his chest. "I've cried my last tear over you and spent my last sleepless night wondering why I didn't kill you!"

Her rage increased with every word. Her

face was livid, her eyes wild. "I was becoming reconciled to living alone. I had plans for a business — you had to come and disrupt my life. Well, you've got me, damn you, and you're going to keep me!" She didn't know it but the tears were streaming down her face. "You had the guts to carry on your affair right here under my nose, in my house! Oh, yes, I'm not so dumb that I don't remember this is the house we planned together right down to the blue carpet and the green house plants. You let *her* furnish it! You let her put me in a back room so she could share yours! I should have horse-whipped her. I should horse-whip you. You're an arrogant bastard, Jake! You're a first-class bastard, as bad as they come."

Although she was screaming and trembling and the sobs were constricting her throat so that her words came out jerkily, her voice dripped hurt and desperation. Now that she had started she couldn't stop.

"I loved you! I loved you with all my heart and soul. I never looked at another man. I couldn't stand for another man to touch me. I'm twenty-six years old and I've been to bed with one man . . . you! I've been kissed by a total of three. How's that for a record?" Her temper was a rapid-rising crescendo now. "I married you again, Jake Williamson, because I thought you needed me. For the first time since I knew you, you needed me for a change."

It was crazy, but she had no control over the

words that were coming from her mouth. "I know I'm not street-wise, or even especially intelligent, Jake. I'm just the stupid little sap who was too innocent to know you weren't worth loving!"

She had never felt like this before. It was as if her whole insides had been cut loose. She felt free! She felt strong enough to tackle a tank! She grabbed a magazine from the night table beside the bed and began to strike him with it. He lifted his arm to ward off the blows, but said nothing. She hit him again and again, her eyes blinded with tears.

Jake was stunned into silence. Finally, when she hit him on the side of the head with the magazine he grabbed her wrist.

"Let go of me, you . . . stupid lecher. I ought to kill you! You've put me through hell, but not anymore. Never again! Do you understand? If you as much as look at another woman, I swear I'll . . . I'll make you miserable for the rest of your life!" She was lightheaded and almost fell on him. "I hate you, Jake Williamson! I hate you so much I'm sick to my stomach, and . . . I love you so much I . . . I could die from it!"

She was exhausted and did not resist when he pulled her down on the bed and into his arms. She cried. She cried with her mouth open against his naked chest.

"Sweetheart . . . babe, say it all. Get it all out. I love you. Do you hear? I love you so much I thought I'd go crazy. You never seemed to care enough about me. And, sweetheart, why on earth didn't you tell me how you felt a long time ago? Sshh . . . don't cry."

A low moan escaped from her lips and she clung to him as if she could merge with his body. Half laughing, half crying, his arms locked tightly around her, he rolled her over him so she lay on the bed beside him. He smoothed her rumpled hair and traced his mouth along the side of her face and kissed her trembling mouth. His whispered words came against her lips.

"You love me that much?"

"And much, much more, you . . . impossible —"

His laugh was joyous against her face. "Try sweetheart . . . lover . . ."

"You, idiot of a . . . sweetheart . . . lover . . ."

He pinned her to the bed and kissed her hungrily, as if starving for her. His mouth didn't want to leave hers even to talk, so he whispered against her lips. "I love you, sweetheart. I don't know what made you change your mind and come back to me, but I'm so glad you did!"

Two huge tears slid from the corners of her eyes. "So am I. I decided life with you would be lousy, but without you it would be . . . lousier."

He pulled away from her for a moment and they both laughed happily. "It was this morning that I guessed the reason you didn't come to the veranda last night," Jake explained. "You had caught Liz's little act. She had on your perfume, darling. I would recognize that scent if I were dead. She touched my face and I thought it was you. I was in heaven until I put my arms around her and pulled her down on my lap. I knew instantly it wasn't you. I know every curve, every line of you. The feel of your breast against me is like no other feeling in the world. I told her she was leaving and if she wanted to keep her job she would take a transfer to Dallas."

"Why didn't you tell me last night?"

"You locked me out. Remember? I thought you didn't care enough for me to make a fuss about it or to throw Liz out of the house." He pushed aside the hair from her ears and cupped her head in his hands. He was going to kiss her again, but she began to talk.

"I'd made up my mind to talk to you. To communicate, as Debbie puts it. I wanted to tell you how I felt, that I couldn't live with you knowing . . . thinking that I was sharing you." She put her hands on his face, her lips trembled, her eyes held a world of misery. "And then, this morning I saw Liz come out of your room."

"I saw her, too, sweetheart," he said after he had tried to kiss the bleakness from her eyes. "She didn't know that my sight had returned in the night. It was while I was sitting alone on the veranda that I suddenly saw the moon. I didn't know what it was at first. Gradually other objects became clear and I got up and went into the house. I couldn't believe it so I moved around. It was true! I could see.

"I went through the house and back out onto the veranda so I could see the moon again. It was wonderful! I got the key from the kitchen and came to your room. I wanted to see you. I had to see you. Your eyes were open and you watched me. I couldn't understand why you were so frightened of me. I could feel the tears on your cheeks and I wanted to kiss them away. I went back to the veranda and sat there most of the night almost afraid to go to sleep. I was afraid that if I did I wouldn't be able to see when I woke up. While sitting there it occurred to me that if you thought I was still blind you wouldn't leave me. Believe me, sweetheart, I was as surprised as you were to see Liz coming out of my room.

He stroked her face and looked into her eyes with a world of longing in his. "I waited, hoping you would fly into a rage, but you walked calmly away as if you didn't care. I never hurt as bad in my life as I did at that moment. I didn't want to go to Houston this morning, but I had to see the doctor and get that damn tight cast cut off and to find out if my returned vision was permanent. Thank God, it is!"

"How could you possibly think I didn't care

that you had spent the night with Liz? I cared! I cared so much that I wanted to kill her . . . and you!"

"I've never had an affair with Liz. I took her out a few times before I met you. After that . . . there was no one else for me. You had my heart in your hands from the beginning."

"Never had an affair?" She looked searchingly into his eyes. "When I left you two years ago it was because I found you and Liz . . . on the couch together." It was not easy to say the words.

"Me and Liz?" His eyes looked down into hers. They were open, honest and puzzled eyes. "You mean the night I got so drunk she brought me home? Why didn't you say something? I was drunk that night, but not that drunk. I admit I was flirting around with her to make you jealous, but I never . . . why . . . that bitch!"

He fell away from her and lay back, his arms folded under his head. "I've been thinking all day about different things that happened. Like Liz telling me that you were living with Dick Kenfield. That was the reason I signed the divorce papers. And somehow I can't imagine the girl from Orange finding me without help."

"You think Liz might have arranged for her to come see me?" She snuggled her face in the curve of his neck so her mouth was against his skin.

"I'm sure of it, sweetheart."

She raised her head and looked at him. She felt as if she hadn't seen him in months, hadn't talked to him in years. At last she was talking to Jake, the man she loved, her husband, lover, the other part of herself. They talked in snatches of whispers between kisses.

After a long, haunting kiss that brought back the gentleness they had lost, Jake said, "By the way, Mrs. Williamson, I never gave Liz permission to decorate your house. I chose the furnishings and had them sent down. She offered to check the invoices to see if everything arrived okay. As long as I was paying her a salary I told her to go ahead."

"I love my house."

"It was a lousy house without you in it, sweetheart."

"Try and get me out of it and I'll . . . break your arm!" She turned over onto him and held him very tight for a few minutes. They smiled into each other's eyes, reading each other's thoughts.

"I think I've got a tiger by the tail." His hand slipped down inside her jeans and cupped her buttocks. "I'll have to be more cautious." He had a huge smile on his face.

"It's too late to be cautious."

"What do you mean?"

"Ain't cha ever heard about the birds and the bees, fella?"

"Are you serious?"

"I think so."

"Are you sure?" His face was alight and he couldn't quit grinning.

"It's too soon to be sure."

"Want to stack the cards . . . in our favor?"

"Sure. Why not?" She grinned up at him.

He cradled her in his arms and kissed her softly, then hungrily while he pulled her shirt from her jeans.

"The door isn't locked and . . . I love you. Someone may wander in from the beach and . . . I love you."

"We'll just have to take our chances and . . . I love you, too."

"The lights are on."

"I know it, dumb-dumb. They're going to stay on . . . forever."

"Forever is a long, long time."

"You bet!"

He raised his head, and the caressing hand inside her jeans paused. A silly grin spread over his face.

"Would you really do all those awful things to me? Lordy mercy! What've I got myself into? You'd put old Carrie Nation to shame when you get all riled up!"

Her eyes shone like bright stars and her lips twitched with laughter. "Hush up! And get on with what you're doing . . . or I'll . . . kiss you senseless!"